Zombie Fungus

Abel's Apocalypse Book One

Bryan Dean

ISBN: 978-1-7352793-7-4

Contact the author via email: CLELUTZ11@gmail.com

ACKNOWLEDGEMENTS

I'd like to thank my friends, family, and you for your support. A special thanks to Darline, Sharon, Steve, Russ, Tim, Charley, and Sean. Without your encouragement, this simply doesn't happen.

To the American Military: Without you standing watch over this great nation, this book may not have been possible. You do what few among us have the courage to do. Thank you.

Edited by Booked for Good Editing
Booked4Good@gmail.com
Thank you for your hard work and guidance.

Cover designed by: Kelly A. Martin
www.kam.design

Kelly, you are a master at your craft!

Image Credits:
everlite1knight/DepositPhotos, Apollofoto/Shutterstock

Chapter 1

Doctor Su reworked the formula and slapped the *enter* key, sending his *HP Z8-G4 Workstation* into furious computations. Glancing over his shoulder, he shuddered. The test rats, piled into the corner of their cage, continued to hemorrhage that disturbing substance.

The sight of dead and dying rats wasn't unique; as a genetic scientist with a focus on viral genetics and neuroscience, he'd been responsible for the deaths of countless vermin. But never in his career had he witnessed an adverse reaction this volatile.

At the test's onset, his trial subjects attacked the control group, devouring them in a piranha-like frenzy. After sating their bloodlust, they retreated to the furthest corner of the cage, huddled together, and began bleeding. Their soft pallid fur stained crimson in a matter of seconds. His inspection yielded no visible signs of injuries capable of causing such intense blood loss. It was as if it simply leached from their pores.

But something else happened, something extraordinary. Grayish-white fluff mixed with the liberally oozing blood. Just a speck at first, then gradually increasing until it displaced the blood entirely. An hour had since passed, yet the mysterious substance, implausibly, still dripped from their corpses.

A notification dinged. His results of the reworked formula had finished. Su's hands trembled as he clicked the *open file* prompt. His time was running short. If he failed to correct the formula and deliver it to his handlers, they would execute his family. Of this, he was certain.

Dabbing at moisture gathered along his forehead, he opened the file and silently watched the spreadsheet's columns populate with thousands of lines of data. A moment later, clarity struck.

He'd been so close and the answer so incredibly simple, he questioned if his mental acuity had begun to slip. The notion dismissed with an incredulous laugh, reasoning that he'd simply missed the connection due to exhaustion.

It was now clear that if the Ophiocordyceps unilateralis spores were removed from the Niveomyces coronatus fermentation prematurely, the spikes essential for proper adhesion to the cerebral cortex would be underdeveloped and free to roam the brain uninhibited, infecting any number of functions.

It didn't fully explain the reaction seen in the test subjects, as he deduced infections would be random, manifesting in varying types and levels of symptoms. The uniformed reaction he'd witnessed appeared anything but random. A problem to be solved another day, he supposed, for he needed to prepare for testing immediately.

The lab incinerator's thick metal gate slid shut, its burn chamber full of rat husks, when the laboratory door swung open. The eternally punctual Doctor Valarie Smith had arrived.

"Su, were you here all night, *again*?" she asked, taking in his disheveled clothing and unshaven face.

Su, after a secretive glance at his wristwatch, smiled and half-bowed sharply. "We have much work to complete. I feel we are close, but also far away," he responded in his usual clipped, broken English.

Smith, now accustomed to the brilliant scientist's riddle-like rejoins, smiled. "Well, I look forward to today's progress review. But, honestly, rest is essential for a healthy mind. Plcase, for your wellbeing, try to get some. Your talents are critical to our success."

"Of course," Su responded, again bowing as Smith walked through the lab toward her office.

He recoiled. Smith would pass his test subject's cage, still sodden with blood and viscous fluff. Su cursed himself for losing track of time. He'd planned to have all signs of his covert test's failure cleaned away, and the lab readied for his workday before it filled with his counterparts.

"Allow me to assist you." Su's sudden appearance at her side, and insistence on helping her with the satchel, full of research documents she'd taken home, was both out of character and disturbingly forceful.

“Doctor! Please, I can manage today as I have every day since our work began,” she said, shrugging free of his grip on the satchel's thick strap.

“Of course,” Su replied, relieved to have distracted Smith as she neared the cage. “My apologies. You are a very capable woman. I meant no disrespect.”

Smith’s features pinched. Su’s actions and manner of speaking seemed... nearly panicked and certainly urgent, but why, she couldn’t say.

“I’m sure you didn’t. However, going forward, please work to maintain a more professional decorum,” she said, writing off his behavior to cultural differences she neither understood nor cared to learn.

Su busied himself with mundane tasks until Smith closed her office door. He grabbed the rat enclosure and rushed to the incinerator. Steps away from disposing of the cage and its contents, the lab door again swung open. His colleagues were arriving in a steady stream tracking an intercept course toward Su. A hard right turn placed his back to the team of self-important scientists, allowing him to remove the sanitation tray unseen and slide the gooey plastic under his lab coat. To avoid seepage through the stark white garment, Su placed the gore-covered side against his chest, slinked past his colleagues, and exited the lab.

The tray had to be destroyed; simply tossing it into their bio-waste receptacle wasn't an option. If discovered, it would lead to unanswerable questions, possibly even a security threat analysis and safety breach investigation. He was here to study treatments for brain cancer, but his CCP handlers had different ambitions for his work, ones he could not allow to be exposed.

Once free of the lab, Su spun in a slow circle, searching for a safe place to store the tray until he was alone. A janitor's closet at the end of the hallway, he determined, would be the perfect location. Because of his long hours, Su knew the cleaning crew wouldn't arrive until after 8pm. He'd be able to retrieve the tray and destroy it well before then. It was ideal.

The closet was tight, much more so than he'd expected. The large cleaning cart, laden with cleaning supplies, took up most of the space in the room and blocked him from fully entering.

"Su," Smith called to him.

Su ripped the tray from under his coat, ignoring the jolt of pain from its sharp edge slicing deep into his chest, and placed it haphazardly in a bucket dangling from the cart's side.

"Doctor Su, are you okay?" Smith persisted, her foot falls audible from Su's position.

"Yes, yes, I am fine," he answered, swiping a towel and bottle of random cleaning agent from the cart. Wiping at his shirt, now deeply stained with the tray's contents and his blood, he spun to face the pesky woman. “I had a slight accident with my breakfast. Made quiet the mess, as you can see.”

Smith flinched at the sight of Su’s shirt. “Jesus, did you spill your entire meal on yourself?” As she stared, Smith thought the mess resembled blood, with large white puffy globs smeared through it. Su often ate what most in the lab considered unpalatable meals, but this mess surpassed unappetizing by leaps and bounds. Avoiding the commentary on the tip of her tongue, again wanting to avoid insulting the man’s culture, she simply said, “Feel free to return home for a fresh shirt, maybe even a shower. We can postpone the progress review until you return.”

“Unnecessary, Doctor Smith. I have a change of clothing in my office. I will be prepared for our review momentarily.”

Chapter 2

Rye toast slid to the left, after spreading generous amounts of grape jelly edge to edge, two over medium eggs center stage with three slices of not too crisp bacon to the right. It was perfect.

Toast in hand, he sliced a section of egg at the yolk's rim, allowing the liquid gold to run freely, but not uncontrollably, onto his plate. With the egg slice secured on the toast base, he added a quarter length of bacon. The aroma, visual presentation, and anticipation... it was nearly overwhelming. This exact combination had taken years to perfect, and he never wavered. If he couldn't achieve this precise grouping... banish the thought.

Since failing his cholesterol test last year, he'd limited the culinary delicacy before him to the second Sunday of every month, away from the watchful eye of his wife, Lucy. And, unquestionably, it was his favorite part of the day. Sure, he enjoyed the time with his brother, Stone, and possibly his only friend, Randy, but he *loved* breakfast.

As he raised the indulgence to his mouth, he glanced up to find Stone and Randy watching the spectacle quizzically.

"What?" he asked, his food suspended less than an inch from his mouth.

"Abel," Randy began, "do you have to eat like that? I mean, we're already done, your coffee has to be ice cold, and the waitress has been shooting us the stink eye for the last five minutes."

"Huh, thought you guys enjoyed our time together. But, hey, I'll just shovel my food into my gut like you two food-vacuums. Seriously, do you even taste anything? I'm guessing, at the rate it flies over your tongue, you don't, but I'm curious, do you? You know what? I don't care. You probably stop when your pants get too tight. So, I'll just get to shoveling and probably end up with indigestion, but not to worry as long as we get you boys home for your chores. Don't forget to wear your aprons!"

Randy leaned forward, concern and anger battling to control his response. "You, uh, um, sure have turned into a nasty prick since you *failed* your cholesterol test. How about you tone it down a bit?"

"Seriously, Abe," Stone chimed in, "if you're like this at home, Lu's going to kick you to the curb. And you're not coming to live with me. So, check that attitude."

Silverware clanging to Abe's plate drew stares and whispers from the crowded diner's guests seated closest to them. "What?" Abe snapped at the table of gawkers next to them, "I'm just trying to enjoy my breakfast; you should do the same by minding your own damn business. And, as for you two," he said, pointing at Stone and Randy, "you're on my list, the short one. I look forward to this time with you ingrates all month. What do I get in ...”

“No rush,” the waitress said, setting their checks on the table and interrupting Abe’s rant. “I’ll take it whenever you’re ready.”

Abe’s head snapped toward the teenaged server, then back to his nearly full plate several times. “No rush — really? We both know that *no rush* actually means *roll your ass.* Do you know how I know? Never mind — just bring me a to-go box. I’ll eat in my car, like a caged animal.”

Lips quivering under misty eyes, the youngster rooted next to their table. Her head tilted then righted itself, like she was having a conversation, or envisioned herself taking Abe to task. But nary a murmur escaped her lips.

“*No rush*, but I’ll take that box,” Abe said, nodding at his plate.

***

“They have meds for whatever it is you’re going through, Abe,” Randy said as Abe slammed the door to his Equinox and tossed the Styrofoam container on the passenger seat.

Abe powered down his window while glaring at Randy. “You just can’t stop, can you?”

“Stop what?” Randy asked, his features strained with confusion.

"Bringing the hurt to your best friend, hell your only friend, cutting my soul to ribbons and on Sunday, God's day; you're probably going to Hell. But I know what's really going on. You're jealous of me, always have been, always will be. You know it, I know it, everyone here knows it."

Randy joined Stone, glancing around the parking lot, searching for the *everyone* Abe was referring to. They were alone.

"I'm going to the park!" Abe exclaimed. "It'll be good to be alone and eat in peace. Stone, I'll see you at dinner tonight. I won't be talking to you, but I'll see you, none the less. Randy, you're officially uninvited."

Stone stood next to Randy, watching Abe drive off. "*God's day*?" Stone said as Abe's taillights flared at the lot's exit.

"*Cutting my soul to ribbons*? He's a mess. When's his next appointment?" Randy asked.

"Lu said it's next month. But, if he doesn't get his cholesterol under control, they're talking about putting him on statins. He'll shit himself if that happens. Lu told Kat he's been working out like a wild man and Lu made him cut way back on his diet. Side effects are obvious. His boss called Lu to find out what's wrong with him. I guess people have been complaining about his nastiness, now HR's involved."

"He's always working out; guys built like a linebacker. How much more can he be doing?"

"According to Lu, he's been throwing up during his workouts. That's how much more he's doing."

They watched Abe cut in front of a woman in the crosswalk, yell at her, then speed away. "Randy, you know you're still invited to dinner, right? If you and Bina aren't there, I'll be stuck with his brooding ass all night. Plus, Lu will bust a gasket if you don't show up. She'll yell at Abe, he'll yell back. She'll yell at me for letting him *officially un-invite* you. It'll turn into a whole thing."

Randy chuckled. "Sure, we'll be there. But we'll be late. Have fun with that."

Chapter 3

Su stood in front of the HVAC duct and unbuttoned his drenched shirt further. His chest now fully exposed, allowing the chilled air to prickle his clammy skin. The relief lasted but a second before the heat radiating from deep within him reclaimed his body.

Swiping at the liquid dripping from his brow, he staggered back to his workstation, called by the centrifuge alarm. The reworked formula was ready.

Taking a seat at the workstation, he leaned against the stiff metal high-top stool's backrest. His eyes slipped close. Sleep tugged his exhausted mind, tempting him to succumb.

A child's laughter startled Su. He knew the laugh. It was his son. But how? Su's family was far away, under the watchful eyes of their handlers, ensuring their *safety* until Su returned home. There — he heard it again. He couldn't find his boy, but his nearness brought a smile to Su's weary features. The aroma of blooming lotus meant his wife, a lovely lotus flower tucked into her beautiful long hair, swept into a bun, was busy scurrying after their son.

Su's eyes snapped open. He'd dozed — a costly mistake. Ten minutes sacrificed to weakness; time he'd never reclaim.

“Foolish, foolish man!” he grumbled as he righted himself then stood.

Su need only transfer the formula from the centrifuge tubes into the vials. With time running short, he’d have to postpone the trials until tomorrow. But the centrifuge faded from sight, then returned. Its blurred edges impossible to grasp as his hand passed through the machine's ghostly image. Su shook his head and pressed his sweaty palms against his eyes. Their heat so intense he yanked them away, fearful they’d damage his sight.

Through force of will, he plunged forward with the formula transfer. The process was sluggish and messy. Much of the formula spilled to the floor as shaky hands repeatedly missed the transfer funnel. But, despite his struggle, Su secured three full vials. Enough for testing, but he’d have to be efficient with its use.

A clang of metal against wood startled Su. He glanced at his watch: 3am. His colleagues weren’t due for three hours. Who was entering the lab?

“Oh, sorry, doc. I thought the place was empty. I’ll come back.”

“Why are you in the lab? It’s off limits, authorized persons only. You’re only supposed to clean common areas,” Su slurred.

“We come once a month for a deep clean. I’m Seth. You’ve seen me before,” the cleaning man answered, squinting at Su.

"You feeling okay, doc? You look ah, ah little — sickly. Can I get you some water?"

Su's deteriorating vision locked on the bucket he'd used to dispose of the sanitation tray covered in the vile liquid spewed by his test rats. He'd forgotten to retrieve it. The mop handle jutting from it indicated the liquid and tray had been dealt with by the cleaning crew.

Seth followed Su's gaze. He was definitely staring at the bucket. "Was that your tray?"

Su's eyes narrowed, he heard words, but couldn't connect the dots.

"Well, doc, next time be more careful. Took twenty minutes to flush that crap from my bucket. Damn near clogged the floor drain. That white stuff... just didn't want to go. Your tray's still in the closet. I'll get it in a sec."

Su's hand found the workstation's edge and held tight. The slow spin of the lab had thrown him off balance.

A hand on his shoulder startled Su. "Doc, why don't you take a seat. I'm gonna get you some water. Damn, you're boiling hot," said the shadowy form, guiding him to the stool.

Seth backed away slowly from Su, worried he'd slip from his perch.

When Seth returned to the lab, he was stunned to find the odd little man walking about the area. He still looked dreadful, but seemed to have experienced a remarkable recovery.

"Doc, I've got your water — and your nasty tray." Seth recoiled when Su turned to face him and he stared into the doctor's dark black eyes.

Chapter 4

Later That Morning

Su sat quietly as his mind raged against Smith's words. They were wrong, twisted! From behind his dark sunglasses, tears breached his eyes, tracing a path along the side of his nose. He dabbed at them with the tissue balled in his fist. His reaction was shameful and dishonored his family, country, and achievements. But it no longer mattered; those things were now dead to him.

"Doctor Su, do you need a moment to gather your emotions?"

Su shook his head vigorously. "No, please continue. I'm merely experiencing mild side effects from my pupil dilation — I should have scheduled my eye exam later in the day. I apologize for the disruption."

Smith nodded and continued to address the collection of the world's greatest minds. "As I was saying, funding for the International Medical Research Exchange has been discontinued. Our study results must be transferred to the SharePoint Portal by noon tomorrow." Smith paused. The work they'd done, the progress they'd made, all of it lost to the greed of people woefully ill-equipped to guide this initiative.

“Submit unfinished test results, *as is*. Please, I implore you to follow our reporting protocols. We may be granted the opportunity to revisit this worthy initiative. Losing what work you’ve accomplished to date would be devastating.”

***

In the alleyway outside the nondescript building on West End Avenue, only blocks from Central Park, a fluffy white substance pushed through a hairline crack in the building’s external drainpipe. Just a dribble at first, the liquid fought its way through with increasing force, pressed forward by a growing blockage where the drainpipe emptied into the city’s sewers.

***

Su patted his lab coat pocket. Glass clinking reassured him that the results of his work remained intact. *President Zi will be pleased.* He passed his colleagues as they scurried about, working to dismantle their workstations and secure their notes, stepped around the abandoned janitor’s cart, and slipped into the hall.

Su had never risked a call from inside the building. But the urgency demanded he breach protocol; consequences be damned. He scanned his surroundings. His search for a secure location ended as the janitor’s closet came into view.

Two steps from the door, Su removed the *Blackphone Privy* from his pocket. The encrypted phone appeared hazy, but he recognized his sight was clearing. He hoped it had improved enough to allow him to operate the device, his singular connection to his homeland.

The phone vibrated as Su touched the door handle. The sensation startled him. It's intensity like nothing he'd ever experienced, as if his entire body joined the pulsation.

He pushed into the dark closet and answered the call from his handler. Refraining from turning on the light, he waited in darkness for the man to speak.

"What have you done?"

"Please excuse my ignorance, but I am unsure of what you have asked?"

"President Zi has been in urgent discussions with the Americans. They have discovered your illegal research. Your unsanctioned folly has created an international incident. It shocked us to hear of your intent to create a biological weapon. A super soldier? Su, why on earth would you attempt such a dastardly creation?"

Su's chin sagged to his chest. His country had betrayed and sacrificed him. "Sir, please apologize to President Zi and my family for the shame I have brought them. May I request to return home? I prefer my punishment be administered by those I have embarrassed."

"You are a wanted man. The Americans have dispatched their Federal Bureau of Investigation to detain you. You will not return home. Have I been clear? You are a fugitive."

"My family, sir. What will happen to my family?"

Su's shoulders trembled as sobs wracked his body. The call had ended. His family would surely be executed.

"Who's here?" Su whispered in response to a shuffling from deep in the narrow closet.

A soft moaning, barely audible against the sound of his breathing, filtered through the space. Su slapped at the wall until his fingers finally struck the switch, flooding the closet with light.

A startled yelp escaped his scratchy throat. "You? How — how are you alive?"

Seth didn't answer; his black eyes seemed to plead for something unseen. A step toward Su cast light on the purple-black bite mark on Seth's cheek. Su's memory flashed. He'd bitten the man before strangling him. Although he still didn't understand why he'd attacked Seth, he was sure he'd killed him. Su leaned forward, searching for the ligature he'd left wrapped around his victim's neck.

"You're dead!" Su exclaimed when he saw the thin wire embedded in Seth's skin. This was impossible.

"I'm hungry." Su jumped. The voice was certainly Seth's, but the man's mouth hadn't moved. "I'm hungry." Su's eyes went wide. He hadn't heard the words — he'd *received* them.

***

White fluff crept along the drainpipe's side, inching toward the sidewalk below. A single insignificant drop broke free from the path set by the liquid before it and floated toward the ground. Its journey ended with a splash in the dip of a spoon where it joined the bubbling concoction being prepared by Sampson Jennings.

Sampson saw the liquid jump in his spoon, but dope sickness has a way of pushing worry from one's mind. Besides, in about a minute, he wouldn't remember it had even happened. He pulled the hypodermic's plunger and watched the golden-brown liquid enter the reservoir. The sight filled his mouth with saliva.

Two flicks on the needle, and a slap on his forearm; it's how he mainlined — every time. Draw blood out, then plunge it home, and soon its arms would hold Sampson in a warm, loving embrace. The strands of fluff racing toward his vein weren't a worry. His brain was already smiling.

***

Su's maniacal laughter began as a chuckle. His colleagues had fought valiantly, but agonizing death still found them. He had delivered it to them as a plea for help. He howled as he recalled them gathering around him, searching his body for nonexistent wounds. Their tight huddle provided Seth an easy target.

Now he watched as his new friend devoured four of the greatest minds that ever existed.

Chapter 5

Su walked calmly into the early summer evening and breathed in the city's life, then slammed his dark glasses to the sidewalk. He no longer needed them and he no longer cared. *Better the meek see the monster stalking them; their fear will draw a beautiful portrait. One I will savor for eternity.*

His senses were fully engaged, revealing a landscape painted by his prey's every action. He need only follow the brushstroke's path to that which he sought — human flesh.

"Hungry," Seth pleaded again.

A sharp jolt to his chest knocked Su to his knees. The pain was so vivid and hot it puzzled him when his probing fingers found no wound.

Flesh tearing free of bone, a deluge of screams, the coppery taste of blood thick in his mouth; these sensations crashed into his mind as one. The images they painted were those of death and suffering, delicious suffering. A woman's scream pierced the chaos, then faded as her life ended.

"This one is mine," the voice received was crystal clear. "They are all mine."

Su's mind raced, another like him walked the city. "What do they call you?"

"Sampson. And they belong to me!"

Su sensed it; Sampson was different from Seth, wild and unpredictable, with a mind that sputtered between rage and sadness. *I must find this man called Sampson.*

"Join me, Sampson."

"Hungry," a woman's voice called out, interrupting Su's communication. It was the woman whose life had ended only moments ago.

Su's hands, pressed tight to the sides of his head, failed to silence the voices suddenly begging for food. "STOP!" he screamed, forcing their pleas from his mind.

"Hungry!" Seth demanded.

"Your food is close, but only a nibble from this one."

"Hungry!"

Su's head snapped in Seth's direction. He'd had enough of his begging! "Only a *nibble*!"

"Hey, are you okay?"

Su glanced at the well-dressed do-gooder and smiled, his black eyes glinting in the dim light.

"Oh, my... I'll call you an ambulance. Just — don't move," the man said, while keeping a safe distance from Su's kneeling form.

The man, with his phone to his ear, tilted his head in question as Su's croaky laughter echoed through the nearly deserted street. He hadn't noticed Seth emerging from the shadows.

***

The sun pricked at Su's skin as dawn's light spread over Central Park. The voices of his soldiers spoke to him, dozens of them, each feeding on the city's flesh. He smiled as some, the ones slow to turn, reached him from airports and train stations. Soon they would migrate across the globe.

From his perch atop a rocky outcrop, the sounds of a city awaking mixed with the voices. The traffic on East Drive, to his back, increased in time with the sun's rise above the horizon. Su noticed the heat was approaching unbearable, but remained focused on Driprock Arch. A cluster of his soldiers were hiding in wait for the morning joggers to pass through the iconic landmark. He chuckled at the visualization of them pouncing on health conscious millionaires, ripping some to shreds while only nibbling on others. Tomorrow would be glorious; tomorrow, they'd march on the consulate.

Su went still. Others, the wild ones, had joined the voices. Hundreds of them.

Chapter 6

Abe nearly jumped out of his skin when the door to his home office burst open. His jolting reaction sent a splash of fresh, scalding hot coffee down his shirt. "What the... Lu, ever hear of knocking? Or were you hoping I'd blister myself to death?" he squealed, slapping at his shirt.

"Why's the coffee machine in your office?"

Abe eyed Lu suspiciously; he was entering dangerous territory, fraught with verbal snares and situational blindsides. He could easily find himself repainting the entire house as penance for getting caught bending the truth. He'd been successful at avoiding it, but this situation had layers, more than he could count in the short time Lu would give him to defend himself.

"Got up early, figured I'd get some work done, didn't want to wake you fumbling around the kitchen, so I brought it up here. I'm nice like that." His response was curt and clunky, *not a good start.*

Lu's head tilted. "Oh *really*? Such a wonderful man my husband is. I'm a lucky woman."

Abe closed his eyes. His first volley had fallen dreadfully short.

"So, tell me, nice husband, why are you wearing the clothes you had on yesterday? Oh, and help me understand why you thought moving the coffee machine from the kitchen, downstairs, to your office, six steps away from our bedroom, would be quieter?"

"Well, I closed the door to my office, ergo, shielding my lovely wife from the racket associated with brewing. Including, but not limited to, me walking to and from the kitchen on our squeaky hardwood floors. As for my clothing, as previously stated, I didn't want to disturb you, so I took them from the hamper. It was a sacrifice, but well worth it."

Lucy shook her head. Abe was talking like a lawyer — he was lying. "Abe, you just can't help yourself, can you? I've told you a thousand times, don't talk like a lawyer. It's your tell, like a twitchy eye or nervous laugh. Thank God you don't play poker."

Abe's brow furrowed. "Bit early to be so harsh. Are you like this at work? Or do you save it for your loving husband?"

"STOP, Abe! You were watching those videos all night again, weren't you? I told you, they're fake, just a bunch of internet hoaxers trying to get people to follow their pages so they can sell advertising. And, like always, you fell for it — hook, line, and sinker!"

"Huh, attacking my intelligence, truly hurtful stuff. And I don't appreciate your tone."

"Excuse me, my *tone*? What tone would that be?"

"The universal, worldwide, wife tone. It's like your teachers held you all after class to perfect it. Which — you have!"

Abe's eyes went wide, he'd pushed it a smidge too far.

"Abel Andrew Willings! I wouldn't be forced to use my previously unknown *tone* if you didn't act like a six-year-old. You know, like all men do..."

A scream, coming from Abe's laptop, interrupted Lu's tirade and refocused Abe on the device. A young woman barely out of her teens was running from something off camera. The video shuttered and bounced as the narrator tried, through labored breaths, to describe what was happening while navigating the narrow sidewalk.

"I shot that guy square in the chest and he's still coming... he bit my damn girlfriend!" The narrator stopped speaking, but the video continued as the pair ran down an alley. Abe shook his head. It was a rookie mistake. They'd boxed themselves in.

Seconds later, the video swept around the litter-strewn area. Garbage cans and homeless were barely visible in the dim light, but they were there in force. "No, don't go back," the narrator pleaded. The video tilted skyward, blurring buildings and fire escapes across Abe's monitor in whiplash fashion.

"Sampson," a voice off camera yelled, "what are you doing?" The voice, rattled with fear, continued yelling words that were unclear but sounded no less terrified.

The video jostled back to street level as a tall, wiry man streaked with gore and filth latched onto the woman. She thrashed and kicked futilely. He had her and wasn't letting go.

"Sampson, stop. Let her go!" a homeless man yelled as he charged toward the escalating drama.

"Help her," Lu whispered over Abe's shoulder. "Stop filming and help her."

Abe smirked. *Hook, line, and sinker, indeed.*

"Holly shit!" Lu yelled as Sampson's teeth sank into the woman's throat.

Blood sprayed the charging homeless man who'd begged Sampson to stop. But he continued headlong toward Sampson and his prey. Two steps from his target, the video ended.

"That was some superb acting," Lu said, responding to Abe's smug grin. "But no, Abe, zombies aren't overrunning the world. As much as you'd like it to happen, it's not. So get dressed and go to work. But shower first," she continued, wrinkling her nose, "because you kinda stink."

"I'm working from home — you should too," he yelled at her back as she left the room.

"Fine, do whatever you want, but I'm going into the office. Just promise me you won't sit in front of your laptop watching videos all day!"

"I can honestly say I won't sit here watching videos *all* day, so, I promise."

“We’ll talk about my *tone* when I get home. Oh, and I’ll pick up some color samples after work. I’m leaning toward gray; I think the house will look nice painted gray.”

“Son of a...”

Chapter 7

Abe watched from his office window as Lu drove away. He stayed there a full five minutes. She was crafty; he held no doubt she'd dillydally around the neighborhood, then double back to catch him executing his plan.

"Yeah, you may be crafty, but I'm craftier," he whispered, his face framed by slightly parted curtains.

Sure she was gone, Abe jumped on his maps program and pulled up the satellite view of his neighborhood. A right mouse click brought up the *measure distance* feature. After a few minutes, he had the measurements he needed.

"The hawk has left the nest," he texted Randy. "Eagle is cleared for landing."

"Eagle en route," Randy replied.

***

"So *much* blood," Randy gasped, more than spoke. "That's the guy from the other videos, right?"

"Yep, and now we know his name. Seems ol' Sampson's been ripping through the streets of New York. Check this out," Abe said, tapping away on his laptop. "This video posted a couple minutes before you got here. It's surveillance footage from a building on West End Avenue from two days ago."

Abe clicked *play* and slid the device to the side, giving Randy a clear view from over his shoulder. The footage, grainy, colorless, and dark, showed a dimly lit street with a shadowy alleyway at its peripheral. Movement, hazy and frantic, focused Randy's attention on the alley. Several forms came together in what reminded him of a rugby scrum.

"That's Sampson," Randy said, pointing at a tall, sinewy figure breaking free of the melee.

"Yep. Keep watching."

"What the... It's the girl," Randy said as the woman, whose throat he'd watched get ripped out just seconds before, staggered into full view of the security camera. The dark stain running from her neck to her waistline needn't be in color.

"It's spreading. Sampson's a spreader!"

The video ended as half a dozen people followed the woman, all staggering, all sporting ghastly, mortal wounds.

"I give it forty-eight hours before it lands in Cleveland," Abe said, closing the laptop. "Time is not our friend. We need to prepare."

"Look, Bina already suspects I'm going crazy. And after the way you acted during dinner Sunday, she's convinced you are, too. So whatever wild scheme is floating around that head of yours, it better not include me telling her anything about this," Randy finished, pointing at the laptop.

Abe stared at Randy, unsure if his friend understood the gravity of the situation. “First, that was two days ago, she needs to relax. Second, eventually, you’ll have to tell her. I mean, how long do you think it’ll take before your neighbors try to eat her?”

“Have any networks mentioned the videos?”

“Randy, if you’re waiting for her to watch it on the news... what if she’s at work when the news finally breaks? It’ll be chaos; she’ll end up stuck in a miles-long traffic jam. If she’s lucky enough to even make it to her car. You’ve gotta tell her.”

“How’s Lu taking it?” Randy shot back.

“She thinks I’m crazy.” Abe’s response was sheepish, and Randy pounced.

“That’s what I’m talking about. See, your wife... she’s used to crazy. Mine, not so much. So unless you have an extra bedroom I can use, I’ll be keeping my mouth shut.”

Abe stood and checked his wallet. “Let’s go,” he said.

“Go where? I thought we were planning stuff?”

“We’re going to talk to Ann.”

Randy’s eyes widened; a common response whenever someone mentioned Ann. “Not a flipping chance. I’d rather tell Bina, she’s not as scary... or mean.”

“You’re soft. Sack up!”

***

Abe stopped at the front door, eased it open, and scouted the area for Lu. His mind told him she was safe at work, but his gut grumbled a warning that she may be stalking about, watching him, waiting to pounce.

He pulled a sharp breath then rushed from the door and walk-hopped across the street with his head on a swivel. Randy, too cowardly to join him, sat perched in his office window. His job was to serve as long-range lookout. He'd warn Abe if Lu entered the neighborhood from either of their development's two entrances. It was a flawed plan, but he wasn't about to let Randy just sit in the office enjoying himself and drinking coffee while he risked life and limb.

Two steps from Ann's front door, Abe's left ankle buckled as he skidded to a stop when she appeared behind her screen door. He shifted back and forth, squirrel-like, then stuffed his fear. He had bigger things to worry about than Ann yelling at him.

"Hello, *Abel*. What can I do for Mister Personality this fine morning?"

Abe's tongue searched for moisture as he stared into the woman's piercing blue eyes. Their clarity and intelligence were intimidating, and her mind, even at her advanced age, was as sharp as her temper. Her graying hair pulled into a tight bun in the style he'd learned over the years represented a woman with little patience for nonsense.

"Oh, hey Ann," he croaked.

Ann waited for him to continue, but he stood motionless, gawking at her like a child with his hand in the cookie jar.

"Abe, do you actually want to come into my house?" she asked, with unmasked confusion.

"Thanks, Ann. I'm busy, but always have time for my favorite neighbor," he answered, while following her into her house.

"What?"

"What — what?"

"Oh, for the love of... what do you want, Abel? In the seventeen years you've lived across the street, you've never simply stopped by. So, what do you want?"

"Can't a guy be neighborly? Seriously, Ann, I was just checking in. I haven't seen you for a few weeks. I wanted to make sure you're okay, that's all."

Ann rubbed the skin between her eyebrows. *He's a piece of work.* "Abe, two days ago I asked you to help me drag some *extremely* heavy trash to the curb. What did you tell me?"

She talked to me two days ago? Abe didn't answer; sitting in awkward silence seemed the smarter play. This was about self-preservation.

"You said, and I quote, *what would you do if I wasn't here?* So you'll have to excuse my skepticism when you say you're *checking in.*"

Abe's jaw fell open, then clamped shut. He had no defense. Keeping his mouth shut might save him from a verbal beating.

"That's what I thought. Well, you're busy and I'm annoyed, so it's time for you to leave. Thanks for *checking in.*"

"Say, Ann, do you still have that brother that installs fencing?" Abe cursed himself. The question was blurted and awkward. But she was kicking him out. He had to nail this down. His entire plan hinged on this conversation's outcome.

"Nope, I traded him for a brother that sells used cars — more glamorous."

Ann's deadpan response threw Abe. "What? You traded..."

"Jesus, Abel, are you that thick? How did you trick Lucy into marrying you? Please tell me, because it can't be your IQ."

Abe squinted through the harsh rebuke; *she's opening her own special can of whoop-ass.*

"Yes, Abe. My brother, Jimmy, still installs fencing!"

"Ah, sarcasm, got it."

"Huh, now this all makes sense," Ann said as clarity stiffened her features. "You thought if you were nice to me, I'd get him to cut you a deal. Look, ya cheap SOB, you'll pay full price like everyone else."

Abe, eyes downcast to avoid Ann's unyielding glare, moved to end his torture and escape to safety as soon as possible. "Not asking for a deal. I need a rush job. I'm leaving you my credit card and some paperwork. It has instructions on what to order, where to deliver it, and... whatnot. Sky's the limit on budget, but he has to start today — no exceptions. If he can't, the deal's off."

After sliding sweaty palms across his jeans, Abe pulled the neatly folded paper with his American Express Platinum Card secured to it via paperclip from his shirt pocket, and handed it to Ann cautiously.

"What are you up to?"

"*Up to* implies something negative. I'm insulted."

"May I?" she asked, waving the paper inches from Abe's nose.

"Um, well, ah, I gotta go. Busy, a lot of work to do. Talk soon."

***

"He's crazy, certifiably insane," Ann mumbled as she read the instruction sheet. Scoffing at the diagram, she gripped the paper tight, prepared to rip it to shreds, but stopped, allowing the memories of the grief he'd brought to their neighbors over the years to take control. With a crooked smile, she dialed her brother's number.

Chapter 8

"Let me know when it shows up," Abe said, waiting for Stone to confirm he'd received the link to the latest video he'd found. It marked the fourth the trio had watched over the last hour.

"Abe, you literally hit send four seconds ago — relax," Stone shot back, growing tired of Abe's hyper mood.

"How about now?" Abe asked the instant Stone finished his sentence.

"Got it, hitting play."

Abe clicked *play* as Randy pulled his chair closer to the monitor. The video, posted over a day ago, comprised of a patchwork of videos taken by cell phones, security, and traffic cameras, fluttered to life.

The image of a middle-aged Asian man leading a group of nearly thirty people down 12th Avenue, wrapped in a gore-splattered lab coat, filled the monitor.

"This guy's new. And that — that's a freaking horde!" Abe shouted, tapping his finger against his laptop's monitor.

As the video switched feeds, the man and his shambling followers came into clearer focus. "What the hell! His eyeballs are black," Randy bellowed.

"Look, you two need to settle down," Stone seethed. "Every time you screech like schoolgirls, I nearly piss myself. So, zip it!"

"Why isn't anyone doing anything?" Abe yelled. "Sorry, Princess Stone, I'm just wondering out loud. But seriously, hundreds of people have walked right past them and not one of them seems phased. It's weird, like they see dead people stumbling down the street every day!"

The view switched to a new angle, which showed the setting sun sparkling on the Hudson River in the background.

A red and yellow flag swaying lazily above the entrance to a concrete and glass building caught Stone's attention. "Is that... it is! That's a Chinese flag!"

The horde strolled casually through the bustling intersection of West 42nd and 12th Avenue, virtually unmolested until they came to the notice of a security guard posted at the building's entrance.

With a dip of his head, the guard alerted a New York City police officer, stationed a few feet away.

"Don't do it!" Stone mumbled as the officer exited his SUV and approached the Asian man.

"This is insane!" Randy howled when they dragged the officer to the ground.

"Wow, they moved fast, faster than they should, definitely faster than the zombies in the other videos. We might have a

Twenty Eight Days Later situation on our hands... I'm not prepared for *Twenty Eight Days* zombies. Not even kinda."

"Abe, we never talked about fast ones. Why didn't we talk about fast ones?"

"Oh no! Guys, did you see that? They took his head, literally ripped it off. I gotta talk to Bina. What are we going to do? Why is this happening? Son of a...!"

Randy's meltdown paused as he watched people scatter from the sidewalk. Cars and busses collided trying to avoid the mad dash of hundreds of terrified pedestrians who'd appeared in front of them without warning. Dozens of those fleeing met their fate under the wheels of vehicles whose drivers couldn't stop. Others raced toward the safety of businesses lining 12th, only to find they'd already sealed their doors.

The trio looked on in abject horror as the security guard ran to the aid of the decapitated police officer. What he thought could be done to save the downed officer was a mystery. A mystery they'd never solve because he was dead the instant he knelt at the officer's side.

They fell silent as the undulating mass of living cadavers fed on the bodies of men who'd died protecting others. They were armed, trained, and dedicated, yet proved no match against the unrelenting and vicious assault launched by this new and terrifying species.

“Did anyone else see that guy nod before his... his *followers* swarmed the cop?” Abe asked, breaking the silence.

“No, and I don’t think it matters,” Stone answered, then continued, “but, I have a question, and don’t BS me. How long have you known this was happening?”

“Couple days, give or take,” Randy answered then recoiled as Abe kicked him in the shin. “Ow, why’d you do that?”

“Stone, hold the line,” Abe said, muting the call. “Because, Randy. Stone’s going to be pissed that we didn’t tell him sooner.”

“I am, indeed, pissed.” Stone’s response startled Abe. “You didn’t actually mute the call, Abe. Technology’s still a challenge for you, huh?” His tone was icy as he continued, “What’s wrong with you guys? I have a ton of stuff to get ready, and I’m telling you right now, if I can’t get my hands on any shipping containers, zombies will be the least of your worries.”

“Are you telling Kat?” Abe asked, ignoring Stone’s threat.

“In time. I want to get things rolling first. She’ll try to stop me if I tell her beforehand, and, well, you know how that’ll end. How’d Lu take it?”

“She’s convinced it’s a hoax and still thinks I’m unstable.”

“From what I’m reading in the comments section, she’s not alone. Just about everyone thinks it’s a hoax.”

“I’m telling Bina today,” Randy chimed. “Are you not relocating here?”

“Randy, we’ve talked about this for years. You know I have my own plan. We should test our radios tonight when I get home.”

The lifelong friends were quiet, each rummaging through their visions of what the future held. It was grim.

Chapter 9

Abe stood at their picture window, glaring at Ann's house across the street. He hadn't seen her brother's trucks drop off a single piece of fencing, equipment, or anything else. Actually, he hadn't even seen one of the garishly painted monstrosities rumble through the neighborhood.

"You're on my list, *Ann.* Probably out racking up charges on my credit card right now. I should never have trusted you!" he whispered, envisioning the woman standing in the checkout line at Dillard's with her arms full of designer purses.

Abe knew developing a Plan B was essential, but couldn't drag himself away from the window. He'd rooted in place, searching Ann's house for signs of life. He had no idea what he'd do if she appeared, but was sure his reaction would involve copious amounts of vulgar language punctuated with equally crude hand gestures. None of it would move him closer to securing his neighborhood against the monsters ravaging New York, but it sure would feel good!

A flash of bright yellow jolted Abe. Ann had come through. His joy slipped away as Lucy's best friend whipped into their driveway in her yellow atrocity of an SUV.

"Lu, why's the Devil's spawn pulling into our driveway?"

"Dinner, I told you this morning."

"No, no, you didn't. Do you know how I know you didn't? Because I'm here, and if I knew she was coming over, I wouldn't be."

Abe watched Nichole struggle to retrieve a large bag and several Tupperware knockoffs from the BMW X6's back seat.

"Of course," Abe said through a chuckle, "because putting that stuff in the cargo area makes too much sense."

"Did you say something?"

"Nope, but I think her broom's malfunctioning. Probably won't make it to the front door. So sad."

"Be nice!" Abe startled — Lu had snuck up on him.

"You've gotta stop doing that! Unless, of course, you're trying to give me a heart attack, kill me off young, and collect my life insurance."

"Are you going to help her?" Lu asked, ignoring Abe's oft repeated accusation of her intentions to murder him.

"Negative. Her broom is her responsibility."

Abe and Nic locked eyes as she struggled up their walkway. He smiled and waved, ignoring her contemptuous glare.

He stood quietly as Nic and Lu hugged and rifled through their usual small talk, wishing he was anyplace but in the same room as Nic.

"Hey, Abe, heard you're still watching your cholesterol. I'm so proud of you," Nic mocked. "I thought I'd help you in your *quest* for a healthier lifestyle. So I whipped up a special dish *just* for you."

"No thanks, vile, *vile* woman. You should go home."

"Abel! Nic spent a lot of time making this for you," Lu snapped, removing the lid from one of Nic's plastic containers. "Don't be rude!"

Lu recoiled as the aroma wafted through the dining room. "Looks, um — yummy. And the smell is so, um, *distinctive*."

"We're supposed to have lasagna. I want lasagna."

"Abe, when I said we, I meant Nic and I. You're having this, um this, Nic, what is this?"

"Well," Nic started, bubbling with simulated excitement, "I found some delicious vegan recipes online. Tonight, Abe will feast on cauliflower and chickpea patties topped with *moxorella* cheese and a creamy avocado puree."

Abe's right eye twitched wildly as his head swiveled between Nic and her culinary disaster. "I just threw up a little in my mouth. Please, Medusa, go home and let me eat my lasagna in peace."

"Abel! Show some appreciation!"

Nic's face morphed into a hurt puppy, complete with batting eyes and pouty lips.

"You're a nasty, nasty human," Abe whispered to Nic as Lu retrieved the meal he'd thought he'd be eating from the kitchen. Her sly grin set Abe's teeth to grinding.

***

Abe sat, staring at his meal, glancing up occasionally to watch the smug women shovel Lu's amazing lasagna into their gullets. "Why haven't you tried the patty things, Abe?"

"Well, Lu, I'm taking in the presentation and aroma. I'm thinking when it stops smelling like dirty feet, I'll dig in."

"Did you hear about the terrorist attacks in New York?" Nic cut in, ignoring Abe's slight.

"Not terrorists," Abe mumbled.

"Ohhhh, that's right," Nic bellowed, "it's zombies. I forgot. I bet that's why you're not eating — too worried about zombies grubbing your tiny, *tiny* brain."

Abe glared at Nic. She'd set him up. "So, Lu is nothing sacred?" he asked, holding Nic's stare. "What else have you told ol' dragon breath?"

"Com'on man, Lu's kept all your *itty-bitty* secrets."

"Enough! You two are... this is the reason I didn't want kids!"

"I thought it was because we decided kids are too expensive," Abe countered feebly.

"I'm going into the kitchen and I'm going to pour myself a giant glass of wine. When I come back, you two had best calmed your asses down, or I swear..." Lu let her threat hang as she shoved away from the table.

"Now you did it. Mom's mad at us," Nic grumbled.

"Why don't you take your nasty food and your nasty self and..."

"Abel," Lu interrupted, "did you buy something today, an extremely expensive something?"

"Nope, no idea what you're talking about."

"Huh, that's *weird,* because I just got a text notification from American Express. Seems someone bought a *no idea* worth forty-six-thousand dollars from Home World Fencing."

"I'm guessing Nic did it. Probably stole your card when you two were getting your nails done. I warned you not to trust her." Excitement and fear battled for control inside Abe's mind. Ann had come through!

"Maybe you should call them," Abe said, feigning concern and confusion. "That's a lot of money for your friend to steal from us."

"Hey!" Nic yelled. "You should shut that hole..."

A bright yellow truck squeaked to a stop in the street cutting Nic's outburst short. Abe didn't need to look. He knew what it meant and closed his eyes tight.

***

"Thank you, Mister Willings," the man from Home World Fencing said when Abe handed the paperwork back to him. "We've already started digging the postholes. Just needed your signature to show receipt. And just an FYI. Some of your neighbors seemed pretty upset when we dropped off their fencing.

You may want to call them; seems your communication's got a little crossed."

Abe nodded and took his time closing the door. After several calming breaths, he turned to face his wife.

"Busted!" Nic mouthed from behind Lu.

Unable to hold Lu's vicious stare, Abe squinted and wiped at his eyes. "You and every single one of our neighbors will thank me, in about... soon!"

Chapter 10

Sampson surged from the parking garage on West 46th; he'd reach Times Square in seconds. The setting sun, unable to reach him through the shadows cast by the buildings along his path, would be buried deep below the horizon by the time he arrived at the banquet.

A swipe at his matted beard covered his hand in remnants from last night's meal. His purple tongue lapped greedily at the essence and stoked his hunger, a hunger which grew more demanding with every slap of his filth-speckled feet on the city's grimy streets.

His favorite soldiers, the souls he'd recruited first, were falling behind. They'd been unable to match his pace since the moment his teeth tore at their flesh, but today, their awkward gaits were more pronounced. Their deteriorating motor skills and sputtering minds goaded him forward. The need to expand his ranks was building to a frantic obsession.

Light, sound, and chaos slowed his pace as he entered the city's most famous tourist trap. Sampson's eyes squinted against the harsh glare, his hands pressed uselessly to his ears. For the first time in days, a sensation he'd forgotten registered in his mind — pain.

A raspy growl escaped his throat as a plump woman wearing a fanny pack strolled into his narrow view. Her visor pulled low, and hands clutching bags full of useless trinkets, she was the same person he'd have targeted before the hunger had found him. Blissfully unaware and laboring under the delusion of safety, tourists had always presented an easy target.

Sampson shook away the pain. This woman had become separated from her herd. She picked nervously at sweaty clothing while turning a slow circle, searching for her pack — she'd never see them again.

The woman's eyes widened as Sampson straightened to his full height, exposing his blood-spattered body to the throng bustling around him. But it was her he had focused on, and her reaction told him she would taste like syrup.

He bolted in her direction, a gravelly scream leading him to his prey. Frozen by indecision, she jolted as his black eyes halved the distance between them. Her first steps were confident, but the disarray of the crowd soon caused her to stumble. Her arms flailed wildly, but her grip on the trinkets she'd collected didn't break until her girth slammed to the pavement.

Sampson fell on his meal, but waited through her struggle, letting her fear season the meat he'd soon devour.

Sampson took her throat first, as her whaling was piercing his skull. It had to be stopped. His head snapped back, tugging her esophagus free of its host, when he heard his soldiers feeding.

Screams, angry shouts, and gun shots swept through the crowd like a breaking wave. Something hot stung his chest. The smell of gunpowder mixed with the stench of his charred flesh swirled around him.

Sampson sniffed the air, searching for the location from which the assault on his body had originated. A formation of New York's finest, positioned twenty yards away, became his next target. All but one of the trio stood with their weapons, tracking the crowd, searching for threats. But the one, oh the one he'd locked onto, the man's weapon, still smoking, pointed at Sampson — he'd die last. Sampson would revel in his terror as he forced the man to watch his friends get eaten alive.

The shift happened sluggishly, dozens of his soldiers responded to his orders with contempt, unwilling to abandon their meals. But when they did, they swarmed en mass.

"You are mine," Sampson rattled in the officer's ear. "All of you are *mine*."

Chapter 11

Abe bolted upright, searching for a sliver of familiarity in his surroundings. Recognition grew in time with his clearing sight. He was in the guest room, the place he'd been banished to often throughout his marriage. He'd actually grown to appreciate the room for its comfortable bed and warm surroundings. In fact, it scarcely seemed a hardship to sleep there.

He contemplated going back to sleep, but his bladder rousted him from between the high thread count sheets. He still didn't know what that actually meant, but Lu was a stickler for thread count, and he was beginning to appreciate why.

"Shit," he spat, as the thought of Lu reminded him of their brawl. It was one for the ages. "Well, you'll thank me, but I'm pretty sure I won't accept your apology," he grumbled as he opened the door and prepared to face the firecracker he'd married.

Stillness, complete and utter tranquility, greeted Abe as he walked into the hallway. The master suite's door hung open, the bed beyond neatly made; the room was perfect, too perfect. He found no obvious signs of the screaming banshee who'd verbally abused him just a few hours ago. This wasn't a good sign.

Cinching his threadbare robe, Abe decided he'd get a pot of coffee brewing before going to the bathroom and started for the stairs but stopped on the top step. He strained to hear signs of Lu waiting to ambush him in the kitchen. Nothing — it was safe and time for coffee. Halfway to the bottom, he stopped again. If she's not upstairs, or in the kitchen, where is she?

"Oh, no you don't. You're not gonna suck me into one of your little traps. Not today, missy." Abe backed up the stairs, watching the landing, ready to react the instant Lu appeared there. He could have kicked himself for letting her take the coffee machine out of his office. "You probably had this all planned out. Catch me when I'm weak and cut off my access to caffeine. Oh, you're crafty, but I'm always craftier," he whispered.

A shower would help. It wasn't coffee, but it would at least wake him up enough to mount a respectable defense. Abe managed to walk backward down the hall, never taking his eyes from the staircase, and sauntered into the bathroom.

"Ha, not today, evil woman, not today," he said, slamming the door.

Pleased with himself, he turned to face the mirror. Abe's features went flat as he read the note taped there at eye level.

"*Fix it! P.S. bet you wish you had some coffee before you read this*!"

"Nasty, just unnecessarily nasty!"

***

Fresh from his shower, Abe walked through the house, ticking off the *get ready list* in his head. The fence had been handled. Next was food and weapons, areas he'd prepared extensively in and was well ahead of the curve. But the guns needed to be staged, something he'd have to use extreme caution while executing. If Lu found his arsenal scattered around the house, two things would happen. She'd see firsthand exactly how many guns they owned, eliciting countless painful *discussions* he wasn't prepared to have. Then, after he explained his way around the guns, she'd question his psychological health. That was an easy one. She'd been expecting his mental collapse for years and he'd redirected her accusations with deft and convincing counter arguments on so many occasions, she stopped verbalizing her concerns.

His cell phone rang, offering a welcome distraction from the pressure of thinking through his plan in the face of his unsupportive environment. Abe shook his head when his Divisional VP's name flashed across the device.

"Hey, John, what's the good..."

"Are you coming into the office today?" John interrupted.

"Well, I'm pretty sure I'm working from home nowadays."

"Let me rephrase. Come in, now. I'm *pretty sure* HR wants to talk to you, as do I. And before you even suggest it, none of us is willing to suffer through fifteen minutes on a Zoom call watching you try to figure out how to un-mute your device. So, roll your ass in here, pronto."

Abe didn't answer, a pounding on the front door and muffled voices the cause of his distraction. Peeking through the sliver in his office curtains, he watched a half a dozen people walk up his driveway, joining a larger crowd already at his door. "I should have boarded my windows," he whispered, then added boarded windows to his mental checklist.

"What?"

"Sorry, John, I was thinking out loud — pesky neighbors causing trouble."

"Well? Why aren't you here yet?"

Abe glanced around his office. Sales awards, certificates of accomplishment, and letters from his accounts, praising his work, hung on every inch of its four walls. He'd built a hell of a career and hated every second. "So, if I told you that HR, and you, for that matter, can kiss my royal red ass, what would you say?"

Abe waited through John's silence, imagining the ruddy little man's expression as he vacillated between firing Abe, and realizing he couldn't afford to lose him. He'd always been a jackass. "That's what I thought. I'll leave my laptop and whatever else I find on my front porch. Pick it up at your *earliest convenience*." Abe threw in that last part out of spite; it was John's favorite expression. One he often used to imply his teams were busy doing anything but work. "If you have nothing else, I have to get my guns ready. Oh, and John, you should move your family to that lake house of yours on Kelleys Island. You'll thank me later."

The front door rattled, the knocking taking an aggressive tone. "They look pissed," Abe said, peeking through the window again. He planned on ignoring them — he didn't remember any of their names, so why engage with them in what was sure to be a hostile encounter? But then one of them slapped his picture window.

"Who did that?" Abe barked as he yanked the front door open.

The mob of angry suburbanites recoiled as one, their bravado faltering at Abe's imposing presence.

"I asked a question! Who tried to bust my window? Why are you here? Shouldn't you all be at work?"

"I'd love to be at work, Abe! But, much to my surprise, when I went to leave this morning, I found about a million pounds of fencing blocking my driveway. Not to mention dozens of workers and trucks blocking my street."

Abe thought the beanpole screaming himself red looked familiar but couldn't, to save his life, remember his name. "So, drive over your lawn. If you truly wanted to go to work, you would've found a way. Don't use me as an excuse for your laziness."

Abe's response was the proverbial spark, and it had landed directly on the powder keg. The angry shouts and threats of violence reached its crescendo as Ann appeared in her driveway. From between his neighbors' livid faces, he watched as the woman set up a lawn chair and casually took a seat.

The clamor faded into the background — Ann's smug grin consumed Abe's focus. She waved then cupped her ear, pretending to listen to the fuming taking place thirty yards away. Abe locked eyes with her and, in a childlike fit, waved a fist at her. His face grew hot when she cut loose an exaggerated belly laugh. But his bright red visage had a chilling effect on his neighbors, and he pounced on the lull.

"Look, you ungrateful pricks. I'm trying to save our lives. And this," he said, motioning to all of them, "is why I never let any of you borrow my tools. None of you understand the concept of gratitude. Do you have any idea how much three thousand feet of fencing costs? Do you even care why I did it? No, you don't. You're too wrapped up in your own little worlds. Well, when you crawl back here with your tails between your legs, talk to Lu, because I'm not in a forgiving mood!"

Abe slithered into his house and slammed the door before the paunchy suburban mob could restart their screeching.

With a stiff nod, he revived his mission of preparing his home for the inevitable zombie invasion. That's when Randy called.

Chapter 12

"Hopkins tower this is UA307, originating out of JFK. We are declaring a medical emergency. Request permission to divert and land."

"UA307, this is Hopkins tower. State your emergency and set course for runway 6R. Emergency services have been notified."

"Hopkins tower, emergency is undefined. Has affected most of the passengers. Crew is isolated in the galley, flight deck and lavatories. Some affected are exhibiting extreme aggression. Attempts to restrain have failed."

"UA307, I have notified security. Runway 6R is clear. Taxi to gate 24C."

Controller Mark Jacobs watched as the emergency crews raced toward gate 24C. He hoped the local news wasn't monitoring his radio traffic.

"Hopkins tower this is DL1710 originating out of LaGuardia. We have declared a medical emergency. Request permission to land immediately."

Jacobs called his supervisor before responding. Something wasn't right. "Jim, I've got multiple tubes declaring medical emergencies. Both originating from New York. Should I direct them to remain on the tarmac and not deplane?"

"Hopkins tower this is DL1710. Do we have permission to land?" Mark could hear pounding and muffled shouts filtering through the broadcast. The pilot's forced calm held an edge he'd only heard once before. He'd made his decision.

"DL1710, set course for runway 6L. Taxi to isolation pad 3 adjacent to fire and safety. Do not deplane."

"Mark," Jim began, monitoring the radar from over Mark's shoulder, "UA307 has parked at 24C. Tell the gate crew to lock the jetway."

Mark listened as the gate crew scrambled to contain the passengers from flight UA307. The calm, yet firm, orders to return to the plane devolved into shouts, then screams. "Damn it," Mark whispered as the bedlam grew. Then the gunfire started.

"What the hell's happening?" Jim shouted from the tower's opposite side.

Mark spun, phone pressed to his ear, to see what his otherwise unflappable supervisor was responding to. Jim was on the phone, his features flushed and stressed.

"What do you mean they've deployed the emergency evacuation ramps? You've got to detain them." Jim pulled the phone away from his ear, staring at it with incredulity. "I'm calling a ground stop. Evacuate the terminal... NOW!"

***

The leading edge of monsters ripped through the airport unchallenged, the stragglers feeding on the remnants left in their wake. The Wednesday morning travelers, packed elbow to elbow in Hopkins' main concourse, stood little chance against the stampede of walking corpses.

Those lucky enough to find safety in service closets or backrooms of restaurants and bookstores soon found themselves trapped with others who'd been bitten. Unaware of the danger until the wounded died, then opened their black eyes moments later.

***

Racing down the emergency lane, Officer Jeffries stood on his patrol car's brake pedal, but it was too late. The body tumbling over the hood sounded like he'd slammed into a brick wall. Shaking off his fright, Jeffries jumped from his cruiser and jogged to the mangled husk slumped against the lane divider. The man's suit, tattered and soaked with blood, hung from his ruined form.

When the call came in reporting a disturbance at the airport, Jeffries expected the usual drunk harassing a flight crew, not a full-blown riot. Countless people had dumped from the airport onto the highway. Traffic sat gridlocked as frenzied souls swarmed cars and trucks, displaying a level of violence he, during his twenty years on the force, had never witnessed.

His urge to call for backup faded as blaring sirens approached in the distance. His focus turned back to the horribly twisted body just as the bloody mess of humanity twitched.

“Stay calm, I’m calling for an ambulance,” Jeffries shouted, stunned the man had survived.

He turned a slow circle, taking in the chaos, while radioing for an ambulance. A bolt of pain, so intense it dropped him to his knees, shot from his calf. Jeffries’ head swiveled, trying to find the cause. His shocked gasp echoed through the stopped traffic. The injured man was chewing on his leg.

Chapter 13

"I'm in no mood, Randy!"

"Abe, did you hear about Hopkins? They've shut it down because of a medical emergency!"

Abe's stomach flipped. They were here, and he wasn't ready. "They've closed the airport? Hopkins isn't even ten minutes away. You're sure?"

Abe shushed Randy's response and walked back to the door and yanked it open. "Get your butts home. They're coming! And you're welcome!" he yelled at the few neighbors loitering in his yard. They surged toward him, but he slammed the door before they could even halve the distance.

"Do you have any idea how the fence install's going?" Abe asked, his voice much louder than he'd intended.

"They finished the section behind my house and Jerry's, next door. If I were you, I'd steer clear of Bina for a few days. They tore up her azaleas. She's not happy."

"Sure. Fine. Whatever. What about the rest of the fence? Can you see any of it from your house?"

Randy lived on their neighborhood's outer ring, affording him a view of a large swath of their western flank. The fence would encompass the entire perimeter, sealing Abe and his neighbors behind a chain-linked, six-foot-high blockade. The semi-secluded location of their neighborhood had green space and small wooded areas leading to the main roads, and he was convinced that's where any attack would originate. But his genius move wouldn't matter if it wasn't installed when the hordes arrived.

Abe's jaw hinged open, then slammed shut, sirens were blaring down his street. "Randy, do you have any cops on your street?"

"No, but I hear sirens."

Abe ran upstairs, trying to secure a wider view of his street. Three police cars and what looked like an armored vehicle straight off a battlefield blasted toward his house. "I think it's in our neighborhood, Randy. The cops sent an armored vehicle. Get ready, brother, it's about to pop!"

"Whose house?" Randy's voice jostled. It sounded like he was running.

"What the…" Abe whispered as the police squealed to a stop in front of his house. "Randy, I've got a situation brewing. Check with the fence guys. Tell them they have a ten thousand dollar bonus coming their way if they finish the fence tonight. It doesn't have to be pretty, just installed."

"What's going..." Abe disconnected the call before Randy could finish. He was busy tracking the officers, setting up defensive positions behind their cruisers and scattering the few angry neighbors remaining in his yard. "This can't be good," he mumbled.

Squelch cut through Abe's head like a hot knife through butter. He slapped his hands against his ears. It didn't help. The sound was inescapable. "Abel Willings, you're under arrest for making terroristic threats. Come out with your hands above your head."

Abe startled at hearing his name, that he was a terrorist, and they wanted him to do the perp-walk in front of his neighbors.

"Abel, don't make this harder on yourself. You can't win."

"What the f... win what? I didn't know I was playing a game. Not a chance I'm going to die in jail while zombies eat my family," he grumbled as he approached the window, then slid it open. "Excuse me, officer. What the hell are you talking about? I haven't threatened anyone, I mean, I want to all the time, but I don't. I'm nice like that."

"Abel, you threatened one John Meadows. You told him you were getting your guns ready and he should flee to Kelleys Island with his family."

"Ha, what a moron. Look, I didn't threaten John, I warned him about..." Abe caught his next words. This wasn't the time for honesty. They'd probably put him on a three-day psyche hold if he told them the truth. "Ya know what? It doesn't matter. Just a big misunderstanding. You have my word I'm not a terrorist. You can leave."

"I'm afraid we can't..." the officer stopped speaking, interrupted by another officer waving his radio in the air. "Are you shitting me? The airport?" he said, unaware he was still broadcasting. He glanced to the house, the radio he held, then his men. "Stay in your home, Abel. We have an emergency. We will return."

"Yeah, sure, whatever you say. I'll be waiting. Take care."

Abe was dialing Randy the instant the last police car's taillights flared at the intersection, leaving the development.

"Turn on the news... NOW!" Randy hollered.

Chapter 14

Kathy glanced at the faces surrounding her, careful to avoid eye contact. The bus station's art déco backdrop brought a mid-century feel to the scene, easily transporting her back to the building's heyday. She imagined the concourse bustling with hundreds of people, dressed in their Sunday best while excitedly waiting to start their adventure.

She had an hour to wait before her journey began. For the umpteenth time, the thought sent her hand to her luggage, gripping her lone carry-on tightly. Kathy's entire life was zipped into the tiny bag. A testament to why she desperately wanted to leave.

Her head snapped toward the heavy steel and glass doors as they scraped across the tiled floor. With each arriving traveler, she expected to find Jimmy's face lurking in the background, planning his next assault on her worn body. "You're afraid of your past, Kathy. Focus on the future," she whispered when Jimmy didn't materialize.

A quick peek at her phone proved her mother hadn't recovered from last night's bender. The slurring hag would probably sleep until her next disability check was deposited. It was strange how that worked. Like the woman sensed the bank receiving the funds. She wouldn't notice Kathy was gone until she ran her account dry and needed money for her *medication.*

Kathy couldn't step onto a bustling New York City sidewalk soon enough. Her dreams awaited her in Broadway's shimmering lights. Not the bottom of a bottle of cheap gin.

"Attention on the concourse. Our coach from New York has arrived. Due to unforeseen circumstances, we will delay embarkation of our New York bound coach by approximately thirty minutes. We ask that you remain in the concourse until we announce boarding. Thank you for your patience and for allowing us to serve your travel needs."

Kathy's stomach knotted, then roiled. She had to get on that bus to New York tonight! She had nowhere else to go. Jimmy was sure to have noticed she was missing and that she'd blocked his cell. He'd probably already started raging through the city searching for her. She couldn't let him find her.

An intense wave of heat originating in her core preceded moisture beading on her upper lip. A full-blown panic attack was cresting the horizon. On her feet the instant she recognized the signs, she rushed toward the sweeping staircase that would take her to the balcony where the ladies' room awaited her arrival.

At the third step, Kathy turned toward the red and blue flashing lights skidding to a stop in front of the station. First responders spilled from police cars and ambulances, making a beeline for the passenger loading bays.

The activity only intensified her burgeoning panic attack and goaded her up the stairs. Her luggage slapped loudly against the tiled steps. Its echo increased with each step and drew the scorn of her fellow travelers.

Kathy leaned against the ladies' room door, trying to focus on anything that would distract her, calm her racing mind. After employing her breathing exercises, she used careful steps to carry her trembling frame to the sink. The frigid tap water cascading over her face cooled the building inferno. But her anxiety still nibbled. This attack promised to be a doozy if she couldn’t regain control.

Harsh voices rose above the running water. Something was happening in the concourse. She rushed to the door, nearly forgetting her bag in her haste. She imagined the bus beginning to fill, and a vision of her watching it pull away without her drove her urgency.

Kathy stood on the balcony overlooking the concourse. It now teemed with throngs of people locked in mortal combat. Men and women, desperate to escape the attacks of the new arrivals, had armed themselves with anything they could weaponize.

A man broke loose from a crush of bodies and bolted for the exit. A police officer, standing in the vestibule, ended his mad dash by raising his weapon even with the man's head. Spinning in a frantic circle, the man searched for safety, then locked eyes with Kathy and bolted toward the stairs in a flash of pumping arms and legs.

As he reached the staircase, a man wearing a Yankees jersey latched onto the running man's long hair and yanked him to the floor. Kathy's scream caught in her throat as the attacker fell on his victim and sank his teeth deep into his neck, spraying blood across the checker patterned floor and drenching the attacker in crimson.

A gunshot pulled Kathy's focus to the vestibule. The officer locked between the glass and steel doors wrestled with a giant of a man. A flash of the officer's face revealed a large piece of flesh had been ripped from his cheek. He struggled to free his gun-hand from the attacker's grasp — the jostling sent another errant round screaming toward the door. The glass shattered on impact, setting free the warring humanity it had been holding captive.

Kathy waited until the last of the throng cleared the building before descending. Her grimy sneakers lost traction and nearly dropped her onto the gore-slicked floor. She gagged on the stench of copper and excrement, but swallowed hard against the bile stinging her throat. She had to escape this hellscape.

A camera crew from a local news channel had been broad-casting the slaughter from across the street. The cameraman's light shone like a beacon of hope against the backdrop of death and brutality she'd just witnessed. Her pace quickened, the thought of more cannibalistic attackers lurking in the shadows driving her from the carnage.

The warm, early summer air rustled her long mousy hair and cooled her sweat-dampened face. Through a confused haze, she stumbled toward the news crew, praying they would rescue her from this nightmare.

As she grew closer, a woman with a microphone bent violently at her waist. Kathy noticed the blood pouring from her neck a second before being tackled to the ground.

She stared numbly into the black eyes of the man wearing the blood-drenched Yankees jersey.

"Well, at least I'll be free," she whispered as the man's jaw latched onto her neck.

Chapter 15

"Run!" Stone howled as it dragged the young woman to the pavement. "No, no, no, get up, run!"

After watching the reporter's neck get torn from her body, Stone knew how it would end for the lone survivor exiting the bus station. But still he hoped his shouts would somehow reach the woman and give her the strength to fight, to leave this life swinging.

"Jesus!" Abe whispered as the camera panned the length of the bus station. The destruction was all-encompassing; zombies had reduced every soul in the beautiful old building to human feedstock.

"Look," Randy yelled, "bottom right corner of the screen, that body is moving!"

The trio, communicating via video conference, sat silently as the twisted figure struggled to stand. When it reached all fours, the feed cut back to the studio.

"Ladies and gentlemen, we apologize for broadcasting those disturbing images. Obviously, we share in your shock and grief," the meticulously groomed news anchor held a hand to his ear, his body visibly jolted at whatever he was hearing. "We take you live to Cleveland Hopkins Airport, where we've received reports of a similar disturbance."

Images of Hopkins jostled in the background as the on-scene reporter ran for his life and tried to maintain his footing while dodging stalled vehicles and lifeless bodies. Flashes of the carnage behind him transformed the landscape surrounding the airport into seconds-long macabre nightmares.

"A highly aggressive throng has chased us from our original viewing position. Unable to reason with them, we're relocating to the safety of law enforcement's perimeter. I'm at a loss to explain what I've witnessed, other than to say it's simply the most horrific thing I've ever seen. We've watched dozens of unsuspecting motorists, trapped in the endless traffic jam, dragged from their vehicles and, sometimes, ripped limb from limb, then consumed by their attackers."

"Hey, those are the cops that tried to arrest me!" Abe yelled as the news crew huddled behind an armored vehicle, joining a mix of twenty or more civilians and police officers.

"Arrest you?" Stone questioned, his features wrinkled and distorted in the small viewing- window.

"Long story, but you're related to a terrorist. I hope John gets eaten first."

Screams and shouted confusion refocused the trio on the video feed. The camera angle had shifted. It appeared as though the device's operator was filming from the ground. Feet and lower legs of the clustered mass scrabbled back and forth as a large red puddle oozed into view.

The feed cut as the brutalized face of the on-scene reporter slammed to the pavement. His dull eyes stared blankly into the camera then slid from view.

The newsroom reappeared, but the anchor had vanished. The eerie image displaced by the colorful bars signaling technical difficulties before the screen faded to black.

Abe raised a finger, asking Randy to stop talking while dialing Lu. “Go online, pick any local news site. I’ll wait.

“Why?” Lu asked, her aggravation with Abe unrestrained.

“Oh Jesus, just do it,” Abe shot back matching her annoyance.

The tapping of keys and a couple of mouse clicks filtered through to Abe, then Lu’s sharp breath. “Holy... Abe, I’m telling you right now. If you had anything to do with this, I’ll shoot you — do you understand? I’ll shoot you!”

“Sure, I created a virus that brings people back from the dead. Now you know what I’ve been doing in the garage.”

Panicked voices shifted through the call as Lu’s co-workers became aware of the happenings outside their office doors. “Abe, I’m coming home.”

“From this second, keep your gun in your hand. Do you remember the rally points we talked about, in case you get jammed up?”

“Back parking lot at City View, Ridgewood, and the Nature Center.”

Abe smiled. She'd listened, even as she dismissed him as crazy. She'd actually listened. "Get moving. Call if anything slows you down. See you in twenty!"

Abe rejoined the video and nodded. "Stone, we'll talk every three hours from this point forward. Randy, meet me by the fence crew. We've got to keep them onsite until they finish. Let's do this!"

Chapter 16

"I think you scared them," Randy said as the fence installation crew scrambled for cover.

"Me? With all those guns you've strapped to your body, you look like a maniac porcupine! Seriously, when I said kit up, I didn't mean bring your entire arsenal."

The crew didn't budge from cover, instead they *volunteered* one poor SOB to check on the armed men. His head popped up, eyes went wide, then slunk back behind the tool truck.

"Relax ya wussies, we're going to the, um, range. How's the fence coming along?"

The crew's lookout crept from behind the truck but remained close, giving himself a clear path to safety if the wannabe soldiers went rogue and opened fire. "We have a question, Mister Willings. How do you plan on paying that bonus you promised?"

Abe, after slapping all seventeen pockets of his tactical ensemble, whipped his wallet out and waved his American Express in the air. "I'll pay five grand now, and *fifteen* grand when you finish. That's double the original bonus amount. Also, call me Abe."

Abe glanced at the crew slowly joining their reluctant spokesperson. The sheer number of workers dedicated to the project was impressive. He moved to sweeten the deal. "Tell ya what. Seeing the size of your crew, and the rushed nature of the job, I'll pay five grand now and *twenty* when you finish, but only if you finish tonight. Deal?"

"Well, Abe, seeing we only have three hundred feet left, I'll take that deal. Your fence will be done by dinnertime."

"Nice! Are you Ann's brother?"

"Nope, he's at her house, eating lunch. I'm the jobsite foreman. I can answer any questions you have."

"How the hell did his sister get so nasty?"

"Um, you'll have to ask him," the foreman answered, thrown by the off-topic question.

"Ah, then you should have said, 'I can answer some of your questions.' Lesson learned."

***

Abe shook the fence like he was trying to escape from prison. It held. Some of the posts were a tad spongy, but would firm up as the concrete hardened. It wasn't pretty, but it was up and would hold until they had time to construct a more secure perimeter.

"I can't believe you pulled this off, Abe."

"Honestly, I can't believe it either. Apparently, Ann's brother is as bullheaded as she is because I'm pretty sure most contractors would have folded under all the whining our ungrateful neighbors were doing. The money helped, too."

"What's your plan when the bill shows up?"

"Ha, it won't. Life as we know it ends today. It all ends today." Abe's eyes glazed over, thinking about the horrors to come. Maybe he wasn't as ready for the apocalypse as he'd thought?

Randy's mitt-sized hand fell on Abe's shoulder. The lifelong friends shared a rare solemn moment. Their lives were forever changed.

As Abe spun to face Randy, a car screamed past, power-slid into a driveway a few houses away, and disappeared into the garage.

"You thinking what I'm thinking, Randy?"

"Yep, eventually we'll be going door to door. That should be ugly."

"I've got an idea. You in?"

"No. You never have good ideas."

"What, you're not even curious? You're soft, man, like a, ah — baby's butt or a pink bunny. Or a baby bunny's pink butt."

"Still no, Abe."

Abe's phone buzzed, interrupting his attempt to strong arm Randy, and after patting sixteen of the seventeen *tactical* pockets, he pulled it free. His heart skipped when the caller ID flashed.

"Abe, I'm trapped!"

Abe's knees buckled, nearly dropping him to the pavement. "Where?" Abe asked flatly.

"The middle of the Valley View Bridge."

"Can you see how much eastbound traffic I'll be dealing with?"

"They're packed. Abe, these things are dragging people from their cars and... those videos were real." Her shrill tone told Abe she was coming unglued.

"Okay, babe. Just stay calm. Lock up tight, keep your gun in hand. Do you have water and...?"

"Why are you asking about water? How long am I going to be stuck here? Are you trying to get back at me for not believing you? Make me spend days and days trapped on the highway? You're rotten — to your..."

"Lu," Abe interrupted, forcing calm into his tone. "I'm on my way. But seeing as we don't own a helicopter, I'm going to be fighting the same traffic you're stuck in. I simply wanted to make sure you have water in case we get hung up."

"I have water. Why are you so calm? It's annoying, quit it. Show some urgency, for God's sake."

"Lu, I'll be there as soon as humanly possible. I promise."

"Abe, stop speaking and come get me!"

Abe stood, staring at his phone. It wasn't supposed to happen like this. They were supposed to be safe at home when the apocalypse ramped up. "Randy, let's go save my wife."

"Yo, Abe, where you headed off to?"

"My car, Randy," Abe yelled over his shoulder as he ran toward home. "How else are we supposed to get to her?" Abe shot back, his words soaked with irritation.

"Hey, STOP. First, I don't know where Lu is. Second, not a chance I'm running off to fight zombies in your car! Third, lose the attitude. I'm on your side."

"What's wrong with my car?" Abe asked, skidding to a stop.

"It's an Equinox, Abe. With a two-liter Eco Tech engine. I can run faster. You might as well ring the zombie dinner bell. We'll take my truck."

"Fine, whatever. But we have to stop at Ann's. We need someone at the gates checking for bites. She's the only person mean enough to make that happen."

Randy recoiled, then angled to squash that visit. "Abe, Lu's trapped, every second counts. We don't have time to stop at Ann's."

The friends shared a knowing look, and in unison, said, "Bina."

Chapter 17

Nic fidgeted in the hard plastic chair, waiting for Helen, the human resources manager, to start their meeting. So far, all she'd done was leaf through a couple dozen papers in Nic's personnel file.

"So, Miss Feral, do you know why you're here?"

"Please, call me Nichole, Nic, actually. My guess is you're gathering some personal information for the announcement."

Helen's brow stitched at Nic's assessment. "Announcement? Please clarify."

"For the Tillman award. I'm the best this company has to offer. I figured I was taking the crystal globe home this year."

"Oh, I see. Well, you're certainly successful. However, your thriving sales results are not the reason for our little powwow. I asked you to join me to discuss your interactions with Adam Stanik." Helen's expression switched to *I got you*, like she'd just ensnared Nic in a masterfully laid trap.

"Stinky Stanik? What's he whining about now?"

Helen recoiled. She'd never had an associate willingly admit to causing a crisis. "Well, Miss Feral, for starters, referring to him as Stinky Stanik ranks third on Adam's list of grievances with your behavior toward him. I'm sure you'd agree that referring to a person as Stinky is utterly inappropriate, demeaning, and, frankly, dehumanizing. It's not suitable workplace etiquette."

Nic's face crinkled. She hadn't expected a disciplinary intervention, as upper management referred to them. "It's Nic, and I'm confused. I'm not getting the Tillman?"

"I'm sure your *sales* performance warrants being rewarded. But I'm not involved in the selection process. Tillman aside, do you recall telling Adam, and I quote, *I'll stomp your ass like every weasel I've had the misfortune of finding rummaging in my trash*?"

Nic stifled a laugh. She remembered, and her description of Stinky was accurate. "I know not of what you speak, Helen. He must have me confused with someone else. Nonetheless, he is a trash digging weasel."

"Miss Feral, that's wholly unacceptable. We're in a position..."

"*It's Nic*, and why is it unacceptable? Don't weasels rummage through trash? I should have gone with rat — right? They all rummage through trash. You're right, it was unacceptable. I'll go with rat next time."

"*Miss Feral*, STOP! You'll do no such thing! Actually, you'll be taking a, um, a *leave*."

Nic tilted her head and, with narrowed eyes, said, "Leave? I don't have a vacation scheduled. Are you sure I'm the person you wanted to talk to? Maybe you and Stinky both have me confused with someone else? Oh, and for the last time, it's *Nic*."

"Oh Jesu... I'm trying to be nice — but apparently, nuance is lost on you. You're being suspended, without pay. We wanted to terminate your employment, but it seems you've made a positive impression on the right people."

***

Nic, after explaining in granular detail why Helen and her entire department were simultaneously useless and hated, left the woman to her sobbing.

"You can't handle the smoke I'm bringing — get a different job, *Helen*," she mumbled while slapping the elevator's down button. "Next time, you'll get my name right, or I'll throw so many hands you'll think you're in a Rocky movie!"

Nic noticed her co-workers affording her a wide berth and nearly spraining their necks to avoid eye contact. The word was out. Nic had come unhinged.

"What? You all think I've never been called unhinged? Please! Every boyfriend I've had thinks I'm crazy. You're all soft!" she yelled, scattering the brave souls who'd dared to come within three feet of her.

***

The parking garage's cool air didn't chill her anger. If anything, it stoked her simmering fury. She hated being cold! "You know what? I don't need this shit. I'm done playing corporate games and pandering to thin-skinned *rats*. Time to take my show on the road!"

Nic rummaged through her messenger bag, probing its depths for her phone, and growing more enraged with every passing second of failure. She had to call her divisional vice president and tell him to shove it before rational thoughts regained control and allowed her to accept her circumstance.

A raspy groan and scraping steps pulled Nic's attention to the narrow space between two full sized SUVs. Nic's athletic frame coiled, ready to strike the shadowy threat. "What did you say, pervert?"

A form, filthy and hobbled, emerged from the shadows. Black eyes locked onto Nic as the dreg of humanity limped from the gloom into the garage's muted light.

"Oh, you want some of this? Well, come get it — ass-hat!"

Her harsh tone and aggressive posture had no effect on the man. With one stride back, Nic created a fair amount of distance between her and the approaching mess. But she wasn't about to run. "Wrong woman, wrong day — perv!"

Nic's eyes remained locked on him as she bent slightly to set her bag on the garage deck. That's when she noticed the blood dripping from his hand. "Ha, looks like you already tried this and got whooped. Aww, poor baby, do you need your mama?"

Nic took a fighter's stance and quickly determined the exact spot she'd launch her attack. One step, then another, and he'd reached it, prompting Nic to snap off a right jab the instant his foot crossed her invisible red line. His head rolled, but still he shuffled toward her. She threw another right jab, setting up a crushing left hook, but he lunged before she could land what was sure to be a devastating blow.

Backpedaling, Nic launched a furious assault. “Oh, you want these hands?” she yelled, her fists a blur as they pummeled the man’s face. His mouth chomped the air, trying to latch onto her, but she was too quick. “You can’t handle the smoke I’m bringing!”

Nic’s hands screamed at her to stop, but she didn’t, instead she unleashed another flurry of punches until an ear-splitting bang drove her attacker to the deck.

Nic kicked the downed man, then stopped and spun slowly after she noticed the ragged hole in his chest. “Who did that?” she yelled, while rubbing her knuckles.

“I did.”

“Get out! Helen from HR carries and can shoot? But you’re such a — church mouse.”

“And you have anger issues,” Helen snipped as she approached, her gun still pointed at the lifeless form.

“Anger works for me. And, not to sound ungrateful, but I had him on the ropes.”

"Sure you did. Your *smoke* was being brought, right? And you're still suspended. Call the police. And don't dream about leaving. You're my witness."

"Witness? I don't think I saw anything, well, except you standing over a dead body with a smoking gun. I'd probably have a better memory if I was still getting a paycheck," Nic said slyly as she restarted the search for her phone.

"Are you blackmailing m..." Helen's bloodcurdling scream startled Nic, causing her to flinch and cover her head, fearful Helen had snapped.

But she hadn't snapped — she'd been bitten. The downed man's teeth were buried gums-deep in Helen's calf. His head thrashed side to side, trying to tear free a mouthful of the HR manager's flesh.

Helen's arm went rigid, holding her gun as still as she could, then sent two rounds into the man's skull. "That's impossible," Helen screamed. "I hit him center mass. He should've been dead."

Helen's face turned chalky. Nic grabbed the woman by her shoulders and gently helped her to the ground. "Just relax, Annie Oakley. I'm going to call an ambulance. We'll get you to a hospital lickety-split. Take deep breaths, and focus on me. Oh, and I was extorting you. Similar to blackmail, but the difference is *nuanced*."

On her feet in a flash, Nic dumped her bag to the concrete, snatched her phone from a pile of useless paperwork, and pounded the key pad. "We need an ambulance and as many police officers as you can send to Thirteenth and Chester, third floor of the parking garage."

"Miss, how far from the bus terminal are you?"

Nic's features twisted with confusion. "We're half a block away. Why does that matter? I have a badly wounded woman and a dead flipping body. I don't need a damn bus!"

"Miss, stay away from the body. Move the wounded to the ground floor. Help is on the way."

A scream from the level below drew Nic's attention to the blind corner ten feet away. She couldn't articulate why, but knew she had to escape the garage.

"Okay, Helen, we're getting out of here," she said, twirling to face the woman. "Hey, are you alright? Wake up, we've got to get you to the ground floor." Helen had become an unmoving crumpled heap.

"Shit, shit, shit," Nic mumbled as she grabbed the unconscious woman under her armpits and dragged her toward the exit ramp. "You're heavy for a little thing."

Another scream filtered from the lower level, the level she'd have to traverse to make it to the ground floor. Dropping Helen to the concrete, Nic ran to retrieve the woman's gun.

"Damn, Nic. What did you do to Helen?"

Nic glanced up from press-checking Helen's Glock 19 and found Phil staring with his mouth agape and saucer eyes.

"Whoa, I didn't do anything. He did," she said, nodding at the dead man.

"What'd you do to him?" Phil countered, baby stepping away from Nic.

"For the love of... Phil, we have to get Helen to the ground floor. An ambulance is coming for her. So clamp that mouth, it's drawing flies, and help me."

Without warning, Helen sat up, her black eyes wide as she sniffed the air. A sound, like sandpaper against tree bark, escaped her maw. Phil rushed to her side as others from the office entered the garage and joined him. But Nic held back, Abe's words ringing in her head. *The zombie apocalypse had arrived in Cleveland.*

She no sooner finished the thought when Helen tore into Phil's neck, sending a fountain of gore skyward.

Nic stood motionless and watched the pandemonium in bewilderment. Phil batted at Helen's mouth, trying to free himself from her jaws. Alison from Accounting fainted and landed on Phil's back, providing the leverage Helen needed to liberate Phil's windpipe. Tim from Design scrambled backward, wiping blood from his face, when his feet tangled in Nic's discarded messenger bag and he stumbled to the ground.

Nic dug into her pants pocket and tore her keys free. Pressing the lock button, she strained to hear her car's horn. The echo made it difficult to pinpoint its location. Dreadful realization struck. Her car was parked a level down. She cursed herself for running late this morning and ending up with a crappy parking spot.

"We've gotta go!" Nic yelled.

Another scream from the lower level spurred her forward. Two steps into her escape, she glanced at Alison's unmoving form and charged the gaggle of bodies. With a fist full of Alison's blouse, Nic trudged, dragging the unconscious woman behind her, toward the blind corner leading to the lower level and the safety of her car.

A hard yank on Alison spun Nic on her heel. Her aggravation morphed to terror as Phil and Helen joined forces to make Alison their next meal. "Tim, RUN!" she shouted as she sprinted from the carnage.

Uninterested to see if Tim heeded her warning, Nic blazed through the parking garage with Helen's gun leading the way. Sirens in the distance energized her pace. Help would arrive soon.

Nic's shoulders slumped, her gut twisting, as she rounded the corner to find the lower level teeming with zombies. Clusters writhed on prone bodies, wrenching free large chucks of flesh and swallowing them whole. Blue and red lights suddenly flashed at the entrance. Her hope reignited. The cavalry had arrived.

Flinch-inducing shotgun blasts echoing through the structure halted Nic's hesitant step forward. Police officers dressed in tactical gear swept their weapons left to right, indiscriminately leveling anyone standing.

"Oh, not a chance," she mumbled and then nearly shed her skin as she pressed her key fob, setting off her horn. She was standing in front of her BMW.

Nic hadn't noticed the deafening silence outside the safety of her car. She was too focused on her phone; only one person could help her, and she was dialing her number.

She never saw the cavalry being overrun.

Chapter 18

"Bina, honey, baby, sweetheart, you have to call Ann. You want our home to be safe, don't you?"

"Don't give me that sweet talking crap, Randy! Why can't you call her? You and your lunatic friend are the ones who want her to check our neighbors for bites before they're allowed into their own homes. I can't believe I just said that — your crazy is rubbing off. And another thing, Randy, I'm telling you, if you and Abe had anything to do with this..."

"Hi, Bina," Abe said, stopping her rant before it turned even more personal.

"Oh, hello Abe. I didn't know Randy had me on speaker. Be careful out there and bring my Lu home safe."

"Masterful redirect, Bina. Points for your effort." Abe had never heard a tone of voice change so quickly.

"So you'll call her?" Randy asked, pulling Bina back on topic.

"Yes, Randy, I'll call her — please — be careful."

***

Randy's F250 bounced and shuttered as he left the surface road and drove across half a dozen beautifully manicured lawns before entering the brush-line skirting I480. Their path would spit them onto the ridge overlooking the Valley View Bridge.

The crowded side streets paled in comparison to the grid-locked highway. Nevertheless, the traffic forced them from the road well before they had planned, and Abe realized, had they taken his Equinox, they would have been high-centered long ago. Especially on the route they took to avoid the airport.

"I got her," Abe yelled while hanging out the passenger side window, struggling to keep his binoculars focused on the bridge. "This won't be easy. We're on foot from here."

***

From under a wild elderberry bush, Abe and Randy scanned the highway, probing for a safe point of entry. Cars and trucks, abandoned by their passengers, sat bumper to bumper, most with their doors left ajar, many others just smashed hunks of metal. Personal belongings skittered across the pavement, pushed gently by the light northerly breeze. Abe recognized this area for what it had become, a graveyard, a static reminder of the earliest days of the apocalypse.

But the bridge was Abe's primary focus. His wife, and hundreds of other souls, sat trapped by the mindless eating machines waiting for them to risk a dash for safety.

"Okay, here's the plan. With those things clustered at both ends of the bridge, we'll need to draw them away. So, you'll break left and work your way to the median. Find a secure position, fire three rounds, fall back to another secure position, and fire three more rounds. When you have them, um, fully engaged, I'll break right, sneak past their rear flank, find Lu, and e-vac her back here. Easy-peasy."

"What?" Abe responded to Randy's questioning stare.

"Well, couple things. I'm not actually *engaging*, I'm bait. I'll remind you, when you watched how fast some of these things were, you had a meltdown. What makes you think I'll outrun them? Oh, and I heard the part about you and Lu getting to safety. But I'm still waiting for the part where I'm safe, or is that not important?"

"Nice. Lu's trapped by flesh-eating monsters, but you somehow made this about you."

"You didn't answer my question."

"I haven't gotten to that part. I'm pretty sure I'll swoop onto the highway, pick you up, and live happily ever after."

"Pretty sure? The highway's packed. I'm *pretty sure* you won't be *swooping* anywhere."

"Good point. But we're wasting time."

"Still waiting."

"Hold on," Abe grumbled as he tapped his cell phone.

"Where. Are. You?" Lu barked.

"Hey sweetie, how's things?"

"Able Andrew Willings, WHERE ARE YOU?"

"Look on the bluff, to the south."

"Oh, thank God. I thought you were..." Lu trailed off, her words replaced by a soft sob.

"Randy's kinda holding things up, but we're working it out. So, tell me, the zombies, were they moving fast or slow? The ones we've seen are just mulling around the end of the bridge."

"Put me on speaker — now!"

"Man oh man, you're in trouble," Abe said, smugly pressing the speaker button.

"Randy, honey, I'm trapped. You know, by monsters. Now, I understand you and Abe are like kids in a candy store about zombies finally showing up and getting to play soldier. But if you don't get your ass down here and save me, I swear I'll haunt you. I'll haunt you every single day until you die. So, sweetie, get over whatever's got your panties in a bunch and SAVE ME!"

"Abe wants to use me as bait," Randy blurted defensively.

"I think he's been drinking," Abe said abruptly as he took Lu off speaker. "So, about those zombies?"

"They seemed slow, unless they were dragging people from their cars. When they did that, they moved like lightening."

"Okay, babe, we'll be there lickety-split. Hold tight. Lu — I love you."

"Why'd that sound ominous? I love you, too, but don't be a defeatist, Abe."

"Okay, I don't love you, and we're going to save you! Better?"

"Better!"

Abe glanced at Randy, a red-faced, heavy-breathing, Randy. "What?"

"You're a rotten son-of-a-bitch, but you already know that."

"We're dealing with slow movers, a good thing," Abe said, ignoring Randy's jab. "You should be able to outrun them."

"Outrun them? That's your plan? You and Lu drive off into the sunset while *I outrun them —for my life*?"

"Actually, I'll double back after I secure Lu. I'll lay down some covering fire and we leapfrog back to the truck. *Then* we drive off into the sunset."

Randy eyed Abe suspiciously then nodded.

***

Abe and Randy slithered down the bluff, keeping close tabs on the zombies at the mouth of the bridge. From ground level, the herd's numbers seemed to double. They formed a wall of walking death, but one that wasn't acting as he'd expected. Everything he'd ever read or watched said they should be shambling around, looking for food. But this bunch wasn't. Signs of the massacre that had taken place were everywhere, but it seemed they knew they wouldn't be able to get at the food locked in the metal boxes, and decided to wait them out. It was a *note to self* moment for Abe.

"Radios on channel seven. Radio check when you're in position, then we stay silent unless it's an emergency. Clear?"

"Clear," Randy whispered.

"Okay, on three."

"On three," Randy confirmed, then bolted before Abe started counting, bee-lining for a tangle of cars forming a 'V' in the passing lane and set up on the hood of an unidentifiable blue twist of metal.

"Radio check. Do you read me?"

"I read. Let's save your wife before I change my mind."

Abe grinned and was replacing his radio when he heard sirens in the distance and growing louder at a rapid pace.

"Randy, hold fire."

"Yeah, I hear them, too. And, Abe, we're not the only ones."

From the shallow ravine just beyond the highway's shoulder, Abe glassed the area, searching for what Randy was talking about. "You sneaky bastards," he whispered as he watched a small gaggle of zombies emerge from the dense underbrush near Randy's position. "Keep low," he radioed to his friend, "the Zs haven't seen you. And I have a hunch those sirens will be coming in hot, guns blazing. Can you cover your rear flank?"

"Abe, they're also moving from the bridge and coming right at me."

Abe swung his binoculars east. The death-wall was on the march. Their path would take them straight to Randy's position. The apocalypse was still in diapers and things were already going sideways.

"Thanks, Lu!" Abe growled under his breath, cursing her for being so bullheaded. "You just had to sashay off in a huff this morning. If you'd of acted like an adult and waited for me to wake up, I would have talked you into working from home. Or sabotaged your SUV and forced you to stay home. But here we are, exposed and facing a herd of flesh eaters. We're *so* going to talk about this later!"

"Randy, find cover!"

"Where, exactly, would you like me to find cover from a three-sided attack?"

"Um, maybe crawl into one of the forty million abandoned cars," Abe said, while tracking the herd from the bridge. They were definitely slow, but oddly focused on the distant sirens. They moved as one, like a team of mercenaries.

He zoomed in tight on the leading edge and gagged. They'd been brutalized. Some had lost any resemblance to the humans they'd been just a few short hours ago. Yet, still they hunted.

"Randy, find cover, NOW!"

Randy didn't respond.

"I say again, find cover." Nothing.

Abe swung his binoculars back to Randy's position and pulled a startled breath. Randy was nowhere to be seen. But several dozen Zs battling one another to get closer to where his friend had been seconds ago told Abe he was still there, or at least, pieces of him were.

"Shit, shit, shit!" Abe shouted as he burst from cover and charged toward his friend. "No, no, no, Randy. Answer me, damn it!" Abe reached the median in a flash, nearly toppling as he slipped on a gooey patch of grass.

"Randy, answer me!" he yelled, his voice strained and hoarse with emotion. At twenty yards, Abe shouldered his Ruger AR, his red dot bounced in time with his stride. He'd trained for this. It was time to shoot and scoot. Slamming to a stop, Abe dropped his red dot on the head of the closest Z. The back of its gore-matted dome exploded as the high velocity round splintered its skull. He adjusted his aim left, the target-rich environment presenting another rotten cranium to his optics. Pinkish white mist hung in the air where it stood an instant before.

Five steps forward, then another stop, three rounds fired. He had to move faster, had to save his friend. "Randy!" he shouted reflexively as the thought of Randy being eaten alive overwhelmed him.

At a full run, Abe let his Ruger dangle on its single-point sling, and drew his sidearm. With nineteen rounds in its magazine and one in the pipe, he prayed it would be enough to clear a path to Randy.

Ten yards from Randy's position, a battle cry escaped Abe's throat. He was close, and he'd made a mistake, but his commitment was complete. It was time to fight.

The sirens grew louder as Abe grew closer to the horde, but help would never arrive in time. With his pistol held tight, Abe began stroking the trigger. Zombies fell away with every round, but the path never cleared. He'd underestimated their numbers, but there was no turning back. He'd entered the flesh eaters' scrum.

His pistol quickly holstered, Abe slid his K-Bar free and took the fight medieval slashing necks to the bone and plunging his blade through skulls as he spun through the mob with skill he'd been unaware he possessed. Hands clawed at him then dropped to the pavement, severed from their bodies. Mouths snapped and gnashed for his flesh, only to be destroyed by violent thrusts of his razor-sharp blade.

The main horde soon became aware of the food attacking them, fighting back, and turned their hunger-lust toward him. With two steps backward, Abe created a fast collapsing pocket, and seized the opportunity it provided. "Float like a butterfly, sting like a big-ass bee," he screamed, and hurled himself at their leading edge, knocking them to the ground where they tangled the feet of the monsters behind, toppling them to the blacktop.

His pistol back in the fight, Abe put round after round through the downed Zs skulls until his slide locked back and a hand pulled roughly on his shoulder.

Chapter 19

Lu stayed curled into the fetal position on the backseat. Its darkly tinted windows did more to spare her sanity than provide protection from the hungry monsters streaming past mere inches away. Whatever Abe and Randy were doing had stirred the zombies hiding amongst the gridlocked vehicles to action.

"Nice, Abe," she whispered, "you're supposed to save me. But in typical Abel fashion, you've made things worse. You best not get me killed!"

A vibration in her hand nearly jolted her to the floor. Without looking at her phone's display, she answered. "Are you close? I can't see you!"

"Lu, it's Nic."

"Oh, Nic, things are — I'm — oh Nic, it's so good to hear your voice!"

"Lu, listen to me."

"Why are you whispering? I can barely hear you."

"Just listen to me, *please.* Abe was right — that physically hurt to say, but it's true. Dead people are, are, eating other people."

"They're zombies, Nic. And I'm never going to live it down. But, I'm..."

"Lu, I need help. Those zom... I'm trapped in my car at work. The police showed up and started blasting anything that moves. The things Abe warned us about are eating everyone the police haven't killed. Oh Jesus, hold on, please don't hang up."

Nic's eyes broke her dashboard's plane; she'd heard a scuffle, and her hope soared as the back of a police officer came into view. But something was wrong. He sniffed the air, his movements sluggish and unfocused. Her worst fear morphed into reality as she noticed the officer's ravaged neck.

"Lu," she whispered, slinking back to the reclined driver's seat, "tell Abe to come get me. They're searching for me, Lu. I don't want to get eaten alive."

Lu swallowed hard then pushed forward. "Nic, I'm trapped, too. I'm on the Valley View Bridge. Abe and Randy are trying to save me. I haven't heard from them. I'm not sure they're even... I'm sorry."

"Lu," Nic said, her voice deep with resignation, "stay on the phone. I don't want to die alone."

Chapter 20

Abe spun on his assailant and landed a jarring left hook, dropping the monster from sight.

"Damn, Abe, it's me."

These things can talk? Abe recoiled. Nothing about this apocalypse was holding true to lore.

"Don't hit me anymore!"

Abe's rage-fueled assault waned; the haze of battle cleared. It was Randy. His friend was alive!

"*Randy*, I'm sorry," he said, his words caught in his throat as he helped his friend to his feet. Staring into his eyes, Abe failed to keep his emotions in check and wrapped Randy in a tight hug. "I thought you were dead, man. And it was my fault. And I don't want you to die. We have to face this together. I need you fighting at my side!"

"Um, Abe, tender moment and all, but we have a problem," Randy said, thankful for the distraction from Abe's unusually human, and equally disturbing, display of emotion. "Zs on our six. They look hungry."

In the split second it took Abe to spin toward the threat. The flesh eaters shambling from the bridge had hemmed the duo in. With only fifty yards of open ground between them, the Zs would be gnawing on their flesh in the blink of an eye.

"Let's do this," Abe growled, sliding a fresh magazine into his pistol, then his AR.

Shoulder to shoulder, the ground they stood on became their red line.

"Hell yeah," Randy said, echoing Abe's desire to open a can of whoop-ass on the horde inching closer.

"On three."

"On three," Randy confirmed then opened fire before Abe started his countdown.

Abe jerked his rifle to his shoulder to join Randy, but a woman's horrified face filled his optics. "Move right," he shouted.

His friend's response was to increase his rate of fire, sending dozens more rounds into the skulls of their enemy. "RANDY, move right!" Abe shouted, his mouth an inch from Randy's ear.

"Why? They'll just follow us. Let's hit'em head on! Get shooting!"

Abe pushed Randy's AR barrel down, then pointed at the cars to answer Randy's glare. "People, living breathing humans, are in the line of fire. MOVE RIGHT!"

"Alright, calm yourself," Randy shouted, trying to equal Abe's volume. "You should've said something," he quipped as they sidestepped right with rifles at high-ready.

"Shit," Abe yelped. The zombies were mirroring their movement and closing fast. He spun frantically, searching for concealment, but found only open space and more Zs.

"There," Randy yelled, then sprinted toward an abandoned pickup truck with Abe on his heels.

The truck's capped bed was Randy's target. On the hood in a single bound, he spun to pull Abe up then scrambled over the windshield to the fiberglass bed-cover, placing them over six feet from the road's surface.

"Can we shoot *now*?" Randy asked.

"Yes, *Randy*, we can shoot now," Abe answered, mirroring Randy's mocking tone.

The first of the flesh eaters arrived as Abe's words trailed off. They slammed their bodies against the truck bed, rocking their safe haven violently.

"They did that on purpose," Abe screeched, as he knelt with his arms splayed for balance.

The truck pitched again as a second wave pushed against their brethren and sent Randy sprawling onto his back. His head dangled over the truck cap's side and came face to maw with a raspy-throated beast. He slapped and thrashed at the monster as gnarled hands clawed at his tactical vest. They were surrounded. Distracted by the force rocking the truck, they'd missed the infected throng that had flanked them.

"Little help!" he screamed when he realized his tactical vest's shoulder strap had been snagged. The mutilated hand refused to surrender its hold even as he twisted hard to his side, snapping its owner's wrist. Steel flashed through his view, glinting in the late afternoon sun, and disappeared from sight an instant before Abe yanked him to safety. Jerking upright, Randy met Abe's gaze, the blood-streaked knife held tight told Randy how Abe had freed him.

"I thought you wanted to start shooting? Stop screwing around and start slinging some lead!" Abe said, holding Randy's stare.

"Yeah, sure, sling some lead. You've noticed we're trapped, right? These things just keep showing up. AND... and they're punking us. You always said they'd be stupid. You, my friend, were wrong!"

"Ew," Abe said, tapping at his shoulder then pointing at Randy. "You've got a little something..."

"It's the hand, isn't it? There's a zombie hand attached to my vest, right?"

Abe's reply caught in his throat as the head of a zombie at the front of the vehicle exploded, spraying a pinkish white fluff across the hood. Then another dropped, its neck ripped open and spinal column severed. They began to fall domino-style an instant later. The rifle reports reached them soon after.

Abe's head swung back and forth, searching for the shooter. To their south, the bluff they'd traversed to enter the highway was void of men or machine. To the north, the brush was too thick to afford a sniper a clear line of sight. An attack from the east was unlikely as it offered no tactical advantage and the zombies had fallen on the west side of their eastbound facing truck.

Left with one option, Abe scanned the sea of abandoned cars and twisted metal to the horizon. He found only death. Another Z fell, the top of its head sheared at its hairline. Abe followed the trajectory and gave a thumb up to the men situated atop the Route 21 overpass two hundred yards away.

"Start shooting, back of the truck. NOW!"

Randy moved into position, the gnarly hand still gripping his vest, and opened fire.

***

Abe sat down hard, his forearms and trigger finger tight and threatening to cramp. A tap on his AR's mag-release sent another spent magazine tumbling to the cab. He reached for a fresh magazine when the gunfire ceased.

"Whew, that's enough to gag a maggot," Randy mumbled as he stared at the carnage.

Abe slumped back, staring at the beautiful early summer sky. "The apocalypse isn't going the way I'd hoped, Randy. Not even kinda."

A piece of fiberglass splintered next to Abe's head, pelting his face with fragments and forcing him to spring upright. He knew what was happening. "Off the truck, now, move, move, move!"

Randy's boots splashed into the viscous jumble of blood and bodies a tick before Abe hit the ground next to him, then slammed his back against the truck. "You gotta be shitting me," Randy howled. "It's like the *Night of The Living Dead* when the good guys killed the survivors."

Abe's Danners slid through muck and gore, unable to find purchase on the viscous pavement until he dug his heels into the side of a headless obese man. "Take off your vest."

"What? Why? Ah, it's the hug. You got up close and personal with these pipes," Randy said, flexing his biceps. "Now you want to ogle the rest of the package. Lu won't be happy."

"She's already unhappy with you. Take off your vest. I've got a plan."

"Your last plan almost got me murdered. Ah, pass on this one."

"Then give me your rifle," Abe said while pulling his tactical vest free.

"Not a chance. She doesn't like strange men touching her. Use yours for whatever crazy nonsense you've baked up."

"I gave you the chance to use your vest. Now, I need your rifle. Hand it over."

Randy stroked his AR lovingly, and held it out for Abe, then struggled to release his grip as Abe pulled it from his hands. Abe secured his vest to the rifle's barrel, inched toward the side of the truck, pulled a deep breath, and stuck the gun into the open, and waved it back and forth.

"Better plan, much better," Randy said. "Now give it back."

"Nope, not until I'm sure they won't shoot us."

"I hate you," Randy whispered as a voice in the distance ordered them into the open.

Chapter 21

"We done here? My wife's waiting for me," Abe said, glaring at the mish-mosh of National Guardsmen and law enforcement.

"Sure, Mister Willings, right after we inspect her for bites. So get dressed and grab a seat."

"You're not *inspecting* my wife's naked body," Abe mumbled as he slid his pants past his thighs.

"What was that?"

"I said, Sergeant *Finn*, you will not eyeball my wife's naked body! I'll check her — ya know what? She's been locked in her car for hours. If she's infected, she would have already turned. I'll call her. If she answers the phone and doesn't ask to eat my brain, we're good."

"She'd probably starve. And that's not how it works. She'll get in line with everyone else, get checked for bites, and released to your custody."

In a quick glance around the makeshift inspection station with its billowing privacy-room sheets, Abe noticed most of the supporting troops were busy either inspecting or guarding the inspectors. Thus, leaving Finn alone to run crowd control. Eyes back on the sergeant, Abe sized him up. He was pretty sure he could take him; actually he was positive. It wouldn't be easy, but anything worth doing was rarely easy.

"I've seen that look before, friend," Finn began, "no, you can't take me. You can try, but you'll lose and look all kinds of foolish in front of your wife. Plus, we're dealing with a, a *situation* which requires my full and unhindered attention. What that means for you and your graying temples is I will hurt every part of your body in fifteen seconds."

How did he know? "You don't scare me."

"He scares me, so get your ass over here, sit down, and shut up!"

"Thanks for having my back, Randy!" Abe said, his eyes still locked on Finn.

"Listen to your friend," Finn whispered, leaning in close to Abe. "He's obviously the brains of your relationship."

"Yeah, well, I'll sit, but not because of your empty threats. I'm tired from fighting zombies with very little help from our well-armed military."

"Zombies?" Finn recoiled.

"*Abe*, sit down before the nice man loses his temper!"

Randy's insistence, coupled with Finn's alarmed reaction to the word zombie, sent Abe to the sidelines next to his friend. "You never have my back, Randy. It's hurtful. You're a hurtful, hurtful person."

"And you're generally unlikable, but you don't hear me complaining. And, if you'd bothered to pay attention, I had your back. Probably saved your *graying temples* from a class-A smack down."

The men sat quietly. Abe childishly ignored Randy as Randy worked up the nerve to tell Abe what he'd overheard the soldiers discussing while he was busy trying to get himself beaten to death. He feared his friend would have a mini-stroke after making a scene, and probably get Randy shot. "Listen up," he hissed. "I've been eavesdropping on the soldiers in the inspection area. This," he swept his hand, indicating the entirety of the situation, "is happening everywhere. It's rolling across the country unchecked. But their orders are to tell us it's a simple medical emergency, and the government has everything under control."

"Under control! Lying bastards, they're going to get people killed with that bullshit," Abe groused, following Randy's lead on stealth.

"Best part? They think it's a fungus, not a virus, a re-engineered and synthesized *fungus*. Remember the first zombie the military shot, the one whose head exploded onto the front of the truck? All that white fluffy stuff? It's a damn fungus!"

Abe's brow furrowed. He couldn't remember if the Zs he killed leaked the fluff, but he'd been busy slashing his way through them, not worried about the contents of their skulls. His body jolted — his battle with the small horde saw him go knuckles deep in Z craniums more than once. He stole a glance at his gloved hands, smeared and tacky with bodily fluids, but a milky-white tinge on his right glove stood out.

"Don't worry," Finn said, kneeling in front of Abe. "It's only transmitted through saliva or deep, open wounds."

"Why don't I trust you, Finn?"

"Probably because... I really couldn't tell you. But, if I was lying, you'd already be infected," he finished, then stood and rushed to corral an unruly detainee.

"Abe, call Lu. Let her know what's happening. Tell her to shoot anyone she's in line with if they even look cross-eyed at her."

Chapter 22

"She works by the bus station."

"Yeah, and?"

"The bus station was overrun. She's in trouble, big trouble."

Abe's eyebrow cocked. Lu was quiet — too quiet. "No!"

"We have to go get her. We can't just let her die."

Abe's forehead rested heavily in his palm. Exhaustion had found him. Frustration was close behind. "Lu, we're out of ammo, the streets are clogged, zombies are running wild, the National Guard has taken over, you're in line waiting to be strip-searched, and it'll be dusk by the time we can even think about rolling downtown. So, she's on her own."

Abe held the phone away from his ear. Lu reacted as he'd expected, with venom and malice. She didn't understand this was merely the first of countless heart-wrenching decisions they'd face in the weeks ahead. Better to build their emotional clauses now and steel themselves for the pain to come.

He brought the phone to within an inch of his ear and moved it away again. She'd just hit her stride. Abe sensed judgmental stares and glanced at Randy. Finn stood just behind him. "You too?" he asked in response to their hateful expressions. "Or do you want to talk to my wife? She's being unreasonable, right?"

“We have plenty of ammo, Abe. I’d be happy to load you boys up,” Finn offered with a wicked grin.

“I heard that!” Lu screeched from the phone's tiny speaker. “It’s a deal, whoever you are.”

Abe’s thumb brushed across the *end call* icon, but he kept the phone positioned as it had been through Lu’s psychotic break.

“Tell you what, Sergeant *Helpful*,” Abe said, inching closer to Finn. “Why don’t you and your boys sack up and go save her? After all, you’re the master of bringing the hurt.”

“She’s hot, so send young guys,” Randy chirped.

Abe’s face crinkled like he’d smelled an overflowing outhouse. “What’s wrong with you? She’s vile!”

“No, she’s hot. Not liking you doesn’t make her ugly. It makes her... normal.”

“So, what say you, Sergeant Helpful?” Abe taunted, waving Randy off dismissively. “Feel like being a hero? Rescue a damsel in distress and whatnot. Because I’m sure as hell not going to save her.”

***

“This is bullshit,” Abe roared, breaking the oppressive silence as they weaved through the congested city streets, barely keeping pace with Finn’s trio of Humvees.

“Whoa!” Randy screeched and yanked the wheel hard to avoid a smoldering heap, which had been hidden from view by the military machines, and bounced them onto the sidewalk.

“Stay on the sidewalk. The streets are too crowded. Like I tried to warn *someone*!”

“*Tried to warn someone*,” Lu mocked, her voice pitched and nasally.

“Zombie!” Abe’s warning was too late. The zombie fell victim to the truck's massive brush guard and pitched the F250 hard-left as its twisted body rolled under knobby wheels, slamming Abe’s head against the passenger window.

“Call your stupid friend. Tell her we’ll be there in five. She moves the instant you tell her to move. She has thirty seconds to make it to the street. We roll at thirty-one seconds.”

“Finn for the big red truck.”

Randy pulled the military-issued radio from the dash and stared perplexedly while continuing to barrel down the sidewalk.

“Wall!” Lu screamed, snatching the radio from Randy as he yanked the wheel left and clipped the corner of the brick wall.

“Go for Lu.”

“Our recon team reported a cluster at the mouth of the garage. We’re adapting our plan. When we cross over Hickory, you’ll advance ahead of us. Slow at the garage, honk your horn until you engage the enemy, then continue east to rendezvous with our recon team on Chester at Krenzler Field. Dismount and confront the enemy. We'll breach and recover your friend. Tell the package to remain in her car. When she hears three gunshots, she is to flash her headlights until we arrive. We also need INTEL on the garage's interior conditions. Get me that information A-SAP. Have I been clear?"

Lu rattled Finn's instructions back to him for confirmation and signed off. "You heard the man, roll ass!"

"That was hot, babe."

"Focus, Abe. I'll military-talk your ear off once we're home. Right now, we need to focus."

"What is it with everyone saying *engage*?" Randy griped. "It's bait, we're bait. How's it feel, Abe? Not so fun when it's you, right?"

***

Curled into a ball, Nic held her phone tight against her chest, willing Lu to call. Her calves inched toward a charley horse and legs stung with pins and needles in the tight space. Even with the driver seat fully reclined, stretching them proved impossible.

The garage had been quiet since she'd seen the mangled police officer sniffing out its next meal. But she feared she'd draw attention by shuffling around to check. Sweat puddled where her exposed skin met the stiff leather of her X6's interior. She needed fresh air, she needed to get out of her overpriced sarcophagus and run for her life, but fear had rooted her.

Through blurry eyes, she checked her phone's display — her battery showed ten percent. “I’m going to die,” she wept quietly.

The vibration against her chest and muted light of her phone receiving an incoming call elicited a startled yelp, which she quickly cursed herself for allowing to escape her parched throat.

“Listen carefully,” Lu said before launching into the plan. Defeat dripped from Nic’s tone as she repeated the plan back. “Okay, sweetie, you’ll hear our horn in about a minute. Don’t give up, Nic, stay strong. Do exactly as I said and you’ll be safe in no time. Also, the military needs to know how many *zombies* we’re up against.”

“Can’t tell, I’m laying on the seat. Please don’t make me look. And stop calling them zombies.”

“Nic, honey, you have to look. We need to know.”

“I can’t,” Nic sobbed.

“Listen up, *Nichole.* Any minute, a bunch of soldiers are going to risk their lives because they’ve never met you and think you’re worth saving. Sack up, stick your peepers over the dashboard, and get a headcount. NOW!”

“*Abel*,” Nic hissed, “I’m going to kick your bulky ass when I get out of here.”

"Good. Fine. Whatever, just get the damn count, chop, chop."

The truck's cab echoed with the sound of rustling fabric, soft grunts, and vulgar language as Nic found the courage to surrender her safety and take control of her destiny.

"At least twenty," Nic whispered. "They're scuffling around like drunks, but keep sniffing the air looking for me."

"Good job, *Nichole.*"

"Abe, you should practice falling down. You'll need it when I get my hands on you."

"Looking forward to it."

"That's why she doesn't like you," Lu said when the call ended.

"I'm heartbroken. Now radio Finn with the headcount while I nurse my emotional wounds."

Chapter 23

Finn watched the gaggle of infected shamble in pursuit of Randy's truck. His plan wasn't gelling fast enough. Every second they sat motionless and exposed was time ceded to the enemy to facilitate a counteroffensive.

He didn't care if Abe was right and they were dealing with the zombies of Hollywood lore. An enemy, no matter their uniform, has one goal — annihilation of their adversary. Finn understood one truth. If he viewed them as anything but combatants, it would cost him his life.

"Alright, let's move," he ordered as the infected crossed East 13th. "INTEL says at least twenty inside. Heads on swivels, remember your training, and we'll be mission complete in under a minute."

Finn craned his neck into the Humvee's backseat. The soldier's bulging eyes told him everything he needed to know. His team was young, inexperienced, and scared to their core. The only reason they were here was because of the VA benefits. He'd give his right testicle for just one battle-tested soldier. But wishful thinking and a nickel still wouldn't buy him a cup of coffee.

"Jones," he said, startling the youngster pale, "you're a soldier. You can handle this."

“On target, Sergeant.” Robins called out.

“Alright,” he said, into his boom mic, “we do this exactly as planned. I’m on point. Jones is with me. Robins and Donovan have our six. Billings and Spangler, your Humvees block the entrance. Eliminate hostiles attempting to enter. Move out!”

***

Finn’s hand adjusted on his rifle’s foregrip, relieving the strain caused by his viselike grip as they entered the garage. “Fast is slow, slow is fast,” he murmured, the reminder designed to keep him and his team from blundering headlong into infected jaws.

His weapon-mounted light swept left to right, searching for targets. A three-round burst was their package’s cue to flash her location. He knew the instant those rounds left his barrel, every infected within a mile radius would descend on their position, so he wanted to make them count. “Remember, headshots or leg-shots, center mass is useless,” he said as they started up the ramp. “Com’on you bastards, dinner’s served. Jones, do you have eyes on hostiles?”

“Negative, sir. But I can smell them.”

Finn noticed it, too — that wicked chemical smell tinged with earthy fungus the infected threw off. But it told them nothing about their ambulatory state. Only that they were near.

Blinking hard and rapidly to clear the sting of sweat from his eyes, Finn missed the slightest movement under a minivan covered in bloody handprints. But Jones hadn't. "Contact, two-o'clock."

Finn spun hard and went to a knee, pegging his light on the struggling form. "Hands — now!"

Black eyes glinted against his light's beam as a raspy snarl greeted him. "Infected contact," he confirmed, then sent three rounds through the crown of the monster's head.

"Contact left," Jones barked, his calm tone speckled with panic.

"Contact," Robins called.

Through the flashing headlights of a bright yellow BMW, Finn watched as the enemy marched from the level above. "Engage, watch your lines of fire," he ordered, his voice firm and confident.

Muzzle flashes pulsed in time with the burst of light from the package's vehicle, making it impossible to get an enemy headcount and spurred Finn forward, dropping infected with each step. Two feet from the package, the driver's door burst open, spitting free a woman with fierce green eyes.

"Down," she screamed, leveling a handgun at Finn's head.

Eyes wide with understanding, he dropped to his knees an instant before two rounds sizzled overhead and sliced through an infected neck, liberating the head it had supported.

On his feet in a flash, Finn charged the woman, who now stared slack-faced at the swelling violence. "Package secured," he said, grabbing her arm and hard-stepping toward the evac point. "En route to evac."

Finn constrained the urge to run, but instinct screamed at him to move quicker through the escalating battle.

"Contact right," Jones barked. His emotions seemed to have steeled as he sent countless rounds at the new threat. But their operational pocket was collapsing. More infected poured from the shadows. Finn had seen it before in the deserts of Afghanistan — the enemy had drawn them in and sprung their trap.

"Fall back! Jones, you're on point. Clear a path. I've got our six. Robins, Donovan on our flanks, package is center. Billings, Spangler, we're coming in hot. We need covering fire!"

Finn turned to cover their withdrawal. The garage suddenly teemed with infected. Their black eyes fixed on the food escaping their grasp. Through his M4's optics, twisted faces carried by mangled bodies quickened their pace. They were going to overrun Finn's team.

With a click of his M4's fire selector to full-auto, Finn issued the order every commander dreads. "Retreat! Move, move, move!" then dumped thirty rounds into the legs of the horde. Shins snapped, thighs crumpled, and bodies fell under the withering string of fire. But the downed were soon trampled beneath their brethren's feet as the trailing infected took up the charge.

Swapping his spent magazine, Finn continued backpedaling, praying his team was continuing their advance. A quick glance over his shoulder confirmed they were, and the entrance was mere yards away.

"Oh, bullshit," Jones yelled.

Finn spun to investigate and caught the tail end of Jones' rifle-stock caving in the face of an infected that infiltrated their blocking team's perimeter. "We're going sideways, fast. Run!" he shouted over the near constant gunfire, then grabbed the package around the waist, hoisted her over his shoulder, and sprinted to the waiting Humvees.

"Check yourselves for bites, then have your teammate check," Finn ordered as the last of his team scrambled into their Humvees. "Call off your status."

The oppressive silence shattered as each member of his team called out, "clear."

"Sergeant, we have an issue."

"What now, Robins?"

"Not a chance we're breaking through," Robins said, dipping his head toward the windshield.

"Son of a..." Finn's words trailed. The sight rocked the battle-hardened soldier. They'd been surrounded by hundreds of infected.

Chapter 24

"That's more than twenty! Not only is your friend repulsive, she can't count!"

"What's happening? How is this spreading so fast?" Lu asked, ignoring Abe's rant.

"It's what zombies do. They multiply like cockroaches," Randy answered as he tracked the horde through his rifle's optics. Lu's head tilted. Had she detected a hint of excitement in his tone?

"Sanders, Comer, what are we doing? We can't just sit here and watch them die!" panic bubbled under Abe's tone as he addressed the recon team with which they'd rendezvoused.

"Sergeant told us to hold position. He's working on a plan," Sanders replied.

Abe's expression hardened, his head swiveled rapidly between the recon team and trapped soldiers until glass skittering across pavement pulled his attention to their rear flank. Dozens of infected shuffled in their direction.

"Nope, not today. Lu, Randy, let's go. I've got an actual plan."

"They want us to wait! So, we wait."

"Randy, look behind us."

"Holy…." Randy murmured. "Abe, Lu, let's go. Time's a wasting."

Randy's truck rumbled to life, and he shifted it into *Drive.* "Well, what's the plan?"

"They followed us to this point, but lost interest as soon as Finn's squad opened fire. So, we're going to give them something to chase. We don't need the entire herd to follow us, only enough to let the Humvees break free."

"Ah, that means we're going to *engage* them. Is that what I'm hearing?"

"Yep. Drive to the halfway point and lay on the horn," Abe said as he jumped from the cab and crawled into the truck bed.

"Um, babe, what'cha doing?" Lu asked, craning her neck from the open window.

"I'm engaging. *So* much engaging — Randy, let's roll."

Randy trounced on the accelerator and sent Abe tumbling ass-over-elbows across the truck's bed before the tailgate decelerated his momentum with unforgiving efficiency. Abe struggled to a knee, grabbed his Ruger, and pushed himself forward the same instant Randy stood on the brake pedal. Abe enjoyed the momentary sensation of weightlessness as he glided face first toward the truck's cab. "Son of a..." he shouted, tucking his chin to his chest and extending his right hand, hoping to cushion the blow. It didn't. His arm buckled on impact then shot straight down, tugging his body with it and allowing his head to enjoy an unmolested path to the cab's steel wall.

Face down in a pile of greasy work rags, Abe found solace that he'd missed the rear window by inches. But it didn't lessen the throbbing in his head.

"Now what?" Randy yelled.

"Horn, Randy. Honk the horn," Abe answered as he pulled himself to his feet, and wiped at blood trickling from his nose. "And, Randy, I think I might hate you."

The horn blared through the streets joined by Abe's taunts. "Let's go you scum sucking pus bags! Come get me. You heard me, come on, dinner's served!"

Abe shouldered his rifle, waiting for the infected to migrate away from Finn's team. They didn't. *Bird in the hand, I guess.* Abe thought as he scanned the infected mob violently rocking the military vehicles. He didn't have a clean shot. From his angle the trapped Humvees sat directly in his line of fire.

"Closer, Randy, close the gap by twenty feet." Abe prepared for Randy's heavy-footed response and braced his body against the truck's cab.

"Hey, are you deaf? I said dinner's served, you ugly bastards!" he screamed; his taunts soon coupled with jeers from Lu and Randy's blaring horn and flashing headlights.

Abe jolted as the recon team sped past, their Humvee swerving wildly through the debris-littered wasteland. “Follow them, Randy!”

Randy plunged the accelerator to the floor and again tossed Abe to the truck bed and sent him rolling on a collision course toward the tailgate. Abe struggled to hands and knees, and peered over the truck’s side panels just as the recon team's Humvee flipped to its side, forcing a fishtailed-stop to Randy’s pursuit.

Sparks and metal grinding free of the enormous machine filled the air as it slid uncontrollably along the pavement, leaving deep gashes in its wake before coming to rest at the infected throng’s edge.

“Shit!” Abe hollered as he leapt from the truck bed and charged headlong toward the disabled Humvee. He heard an engine rev, but his focus was on the Zs swarming into view. “This was a horrible idea,” he muttered as he brought his Ruger to bear and dropped three infected with an equal number of shots fired.

Countless infected converging on the scene drove Abe’s advance. The trapped soldiers stood little chance of escaping unscathed unless he culled the herd and cleared a path. With his aim sweeping back and forth, Abe’s optics landed on a police officer’s forehead. Abe’s excitement morphed to anger when the officer's head lolled right at an unnatural angle. He wasn't there to help — he wanted to feast!

"Time for you to call it a night," Abe whispered, stroking his rifle's trigger an instant before the officer disappeared behind a wall of red metal.

"Get in. I have an actual plan. And we won't have to *engage*!"

Abe hurled his body into the truck bed and braced for acceleration. At twenty-five yards, Randy locked the brakes and drifted into a one-hundred-and-eighty degree turn. The F250 rocked on its springs as smoke from the tires' screeching stop drifted over its hood.

"What's about to happen?" Lu asked worriedly as Randy revved the truck's massive V8 and pulsed his grip on the steering wheel.

"Hold on, Lu."

With wild eyes and a wicked grin, Randy propelled the truck forward, letting loose a rollercoaster scream and forcing Lu's body deep into her seat. "Randyyyyy, what are you doing?"

Her plea fell on deaf ears. Randy's focus on the distressed Humvee was the equivalent of horse blinders. She thought she heard Abe screaming, but couldn't really tell with her head resting in the crook of her elbows and covering her ears.

Randy heard Abe's tortured cries from the truck bed, but ignored him. At ten feet from impact, he had to stay focused on the target. A flash later, he launched phase two of his plan and yanked the wheel hard right, stood on the brake pedal, and braced for impact. The satisfying crunch of infected bodies destroyed by the brush guard's glancing blow resonated through the steering wheel as he slammed the truck into *Reverse* and backed the rear bumper against the undercarriage of the upended Humvee.

"Get them out!" Randy yelled from his opened window.

Abe was standing on the tailgate in a flash, struggling to work the door latch, when it burst open. "In the truck, NOW!"

"Move ass, Abe. We've got visitors!"

"We're good, Randy."

Without a moment's hesitation, Randy launched them forward then squealed through a wide semicircle to face Finn's ensnared team. He pushed the V8 to its limits as they skirted the horde, cleaving through their outer edge and thinning their ranks.

On their second pass, Abe, Sanders, and Comer pummeled the infected with dozens of rounds, further shrinking their numbers. On their third pass, the lead Humvee broke free, creating a gap for the others to slip through.

In a matter of seconds, they formed a convoy and sped from the city.

Chapter 25

Their convoy limped to a stop near the inspection tent at the western mouth of the Valley View Bridge. Most of Finn's troops had remained there, tasked with assisting law enforcement with examining hundreds of civilians for signs of infection. He'd expected them to be wrapped up by now, but they weren't.

Abe was moving the instant they squeaked to a halt, running to the Humvee in which Nic had been secured. "Was she bitten, scratched, anything?" he asked as Finn dismounted.

"Safe and sound," Finn said, stretching his back.

"Oh, well, that's good," Abe said. "You're sure, right? Because I have a sinking feeling she'll be staying at my house for a while."

Finn nodded as Nic emerged from the backseat looking haggard and shell-shocked. "Abe," she said, with a mock salute.

Abe moved in her direction, but Lu pushed him aside, rushing to comfort Nic. He watched stoically as the women sobbed and held back his commentary on the trouble they'd caused. He should be home, preparing their neighborhood's defenses, not traipsing around the city, saving people too bullheaded to listen to his warnings.

"Abe, walk with me."

"Randy, keep an eye on things," Abe said, bobbing his head at Lu and Nic.

Out of earshot, Finn turned toward Abe. "What you did back there was stupid, reckless, and probably the bravest thing I've ever seen. Thank you for saving my soldiers. But, next time, let me know what the hell you're doing. Confusion on the battlefield is deadly. You got lucky this time."

Abe scrunched his brow, unsure if Finn had reprimanded or thanked him. "Luck had nothing to do with it. Sometimes, you have to act. And you're welcome. I think."

"Tell me something. Why wasn't Nic's husband or boyfriend trying to save her? I mean, it's obvious you two, um, have your *differences*, but you were the one she came looking for when she needed help."

Abe grinned. Finn was a good soldier, but terrible at subtlety. "She's single, Sergeant Helpful. So, as repulsive as I find it, you're free to win her *fancy*."

"That obvious?" Finn chuckled.

"Obvious and sad. I'd give you some advice, but I'm tired and want to get home. Where Nic'll spread her own special brand of happiness until I feed her to the zombies. And, I have a question for you. If you answer it, I'll give you my address, you know, in case you want to stop by for a *beer*."

"Shoot."

"How the hell did the National Guard get on scene so fast? This shit's been flying under the radar for a week or so, but only broke loose today. And yet, here you are, fully kitted and ready to rock. *Weird*, don't you think?"

"Huh, you're smarter than Nic led me to believe. Let's just say we watched the same videos as you. And once the federal apparatus latches onto something, well, you can bet money they'll throw soldiers at the problem."

"I knew it! Son of a... I knew the government was covering it up. You have to tell my wife. She thinks I'm crazy. But I knew the feds were waist deep in this mess. So, how bad is it?"

"It's as bad as you think, probably worse. They've already set up a refugee camp in Central Park, few other places as well. We've deployed to the grid and water treatment facilities, but we're already on our heels. Tell you what, give me your address and I'll stop by for that *beer* and we'll talk. Deal?"

"Deal. But make sure you're armed... you'll need it."

Chapter 26

Su enjoyed his rightful place atop his throne of decay. The PRC's Consulate General's office provided him unobstructed views of the Hudson River, which no longer brought him the serenity it once had.

Again, he recoiled as more of his soldiers went dark. The world is shaking free of its disbelief and fighting back. His soldiers had practiced discretion during their hunts, but the others, the wild ones, rampaged through the streets. Their appetite proved insatiable. They hunted during the heat of the day; they were undisciplined fools who'd brought the human resistance to bear upon them all. And his connection to them had vanished.

Another challenge had arisen. His newest soldiers were sluggish, unfocused dolts. Su's grip on their minds had become precarious as they challenged his rule. They were only clear when screaming for the hunt — to feed. They were forever hungry.

The wild ones divided the city, forced their food into hiding, with many more rushing to seek shelter behind their human fighter's barriers, and waged war against his soldiers. Their leader, the wild one named Sampson, must be brought to heel. *He will make a fine lapdog.*

Su closed his black eyes, and again searched for Sampson, finding only a darkness matching his countless other searches. "I must seek him out, hunt him as a soldier hunts his enemy in the jungle. I must end his reign."

Rising from his throne, Su tore a succulent morsel of flesh free from his throne, merely enough to sate his burgeoning hunger. He recognized this pile of rotting flesh must sustain him through the weeks ahead, but was already approaching inedibility. Times of scarcity approached. If he failed to conquer the wild ones, the search for fresh hunting grounds would begin.

Chapter 27

"Damn it, Ann — let me in! This fence, the one you're hiding behind, was my idea. You'd be running for the hills, and probably getting eaten, if I hadn't acted! You can thank me tomorrow. Tonight, though, I need to shower, eat, and get some sleep. I'm tired from *saving lives* all day!"

Ann paced the length of the gate, glaring at Abe through its chain link. This was her chance to rid the neighborhood of Abel forever. But he had a point. They'd be running for their lives if it weren't for his mental illness driving him to have the fence built. Plus, he owned guns, a lot of guns, making him an asset. But he always crawled under her skin and stomped her last nerve! There was no zombie apocalypse rulebook dictating she had to be grateful for the actions of another person, no matter what they did, especially Abel!

"Ann," Lu began, "let him in. If you don't, he'll stand there yelling and screaming and keep us awake all night."

Ann spun on Lu with fiery eyes. "Don't make me regret letting you in," Ann's tone dripped with venom, "go home and take care of Nic. I'll deal with your husband."

"And you'll deal with *my husband* from behind the safety of the fence he was smart enough to have installed. Is that what

I'm hearing? Do you know anything about zombies, Ann? I'm guessing not, but Abe does..."

"Hey, don't bargain with her!" Abe shouted. "I live here. She can't keep me from my house. I'm not infected. She should be throwing herself at my feet, thanking me for saving hers and everyone else's lives! She needs to suck it up and let me IN."

"Why? Since you moved in, you've been a thorn in this community's side. I'm convinced if it weren't for Lu, you'd have been executed years ago!"

"Oh really? My neighbors, who I've never talked to, whose names I don't know, would have killed me? For what, Ann? Not letting them borrow my tools? Or maybe because I don't let the mailman cut across my lawn? I got it, I've yelled at their rat-kids for playing in the street in front of my house while I'm trying to sleep. Sure, seems plausible they'd want me dead! I think you're projecting, *Ann.*"

Abe met Ann's glare as he worked through his options. Of them, shooting her was the obvious choice. But wasting ammo would be a mistake. They'd need every round if they were to survive.

"Oh, whatever," Ann huffed as she unlocked the gate. "Just get out of my sight. And we're having a neighborhood meeting tomorrow morning. Be there!"

***

Abe glowered at Nic, sitting on *his* chair with her head bowed. Maybe he should have taken his chances with the infected outside the fence line. He'd also expected Randy to be waiting for him, but apparently his best friend turned into vapor on a stiff breeze the instant Ann let him in with Lu and Nic.

"You know you can't stay here forever, right?"

Abe recoiled when Nic raised her head. Her eyes were empty, void of the feisty soul he'd sparred with for nearly a decade. The sight weakened him. "I'm kidding, you can stay as long as you need," the words were out of his mouth before his brain could clamp it shut.

"Abe, I'm sorry I doubted you," Nic croaked.

"And?"

"And, what?" Nic squinted, confused by Abe's vagueness.

"He's waiting for you to thank him, Nic. Probably me too. So, I'll start. Thank you, oh brave husband, for rushing to the aid of your frail wife in her moment of need."

Abe's nose crinkled. "That was horrible. A simple thank you would suffice."

"Oh, well then, this is your simple thank you."

"Ah, don't mention it, babe."

"Yes, thank you, big strong Abel. Had you not exhibited unparalleled bravery in the face of insurmountable odds, I would have died alone in a garage."

Abe's head tilted, the gravity of the day's events catching up to him. Over the course of a few hours, life as they knew it changed forever.

"Do you think we can still order pizza? I'm starving!" he asked, his voice hollow and knowing the answer. "We should have ordered pizza yesterday before this train left the rails."

They sat quietly, letting reality filter in. They'd be forced to kill to survive.

Chapter 28

Sampson growled as he tried to receive his soldier's thoughts. They had vanished, and the others were hungry. The lightless tunnels of the city's subway system bristled with rage. His grip was loosening. He needed to feed them. But their food was hiding or fighting back, and he had lost many soldiers as they rooted out the tiniest of meals.

But the one called Su was becoming a dangerous nuisance. He had sent his soldiers to the streets to hunt for Sampson, battling his soldiers as they searched. Sampson ignored Su's projections, begging for a truce, but peace was something Sampson didn't understand.

He tried to reach the soldiers huddled near him, but their minds were going blank. They had to feed. Each recruit grew dimmer, more difficult to reach. *Useless husks*!

Sampson bolted from the herd, setting course for the Fifth Avenue and 59th Street subway station. An action soon mimicked by his legions thirsty for the hunt and wracked by hunger. His sputtering mind remembered the route. He'd followed it countless times in his quest to acquire easy money from the pockets of unsuspecting tourists too enamored with the dream-like wealth surrounding them, steps from Central Park, to notice his hand in their pockets.

This path would end behind the human fighter's lines, coughing his army to the streets mere feet from the emergency shelters speckled throughout Central Park's grounds. The food would panic and scatter only to find the barriers erected to protect them, also held them captive. The food cowering inside their plush properties skirting the killing field, who'd once considered themselves lucky to have benefitted from the fighter's choice for the city's last stand, would find themselves trapped. Their fate sealed like meat in a freezer.

Sampson slowed his pace. What was unseen he heard, what was unheard he smelled. The scent of the fighters guarding the station reached him. Sweeter than the finest perfume and tinged with fear, their meat would be seasoned with a bouquet of flavor.

His pace quickened as the dim glow cast by their security lights slowly brightened. He reveled in the stirring excitement of his trailing soldiers and accelerated toward the fighters. Sampson burst through the tunnel opening and stopped, allowing his ravenous soldiers to overtake him and rush the fighter's position.

He snarled as loud bangs and startled screams echoed from the stark white tile lining the walls of the station's passenger area. His soldiers dropped in waves as he sheltered from danger, but their numbers were too great. The cacophony waned as the fighters' numbers dwindled.

When the sound of flesh being consumed replaced the din of battle, Sampson joined his soldiers. They would strip these bodies to their bones, savoring the appetizer and lusting for the main course.

Chapter 29

Sergeant Blum rumbled through the glass doors of the 20s' era art deco building on the corner of 59th and Fifth, leaving his squad to guard the gate at Grand Army Plaza. "We should have ended the barrier at Fifth and let this building fall to the infected," he mumbled angrily.

Private Devon's face went ghostly white when the youngster set eyes on Blum's hard features.

"Let me guess, Pamela Wentworth has requested my presence at her palace's threshold," Blum barked.

"Yes sir. Sergeant, I tried to tell her, but she insisted on talking to you. I'm sorry, sir."

"Relax, Devon. *Pamela* wants to speak to the *manager* regarding the poor service she's received. You wouldn't have changed her mind."

The elevator chimed Blum's arrival on the 17th floor, and Pamela's private entrance swung open. In three seconds, she would vent her frustration to him and he still wouldn't care.

"Sergeant... whatever your name is. We're running out of food. I demand you inform me when our pantries will be replenished. Furthermore, has the military devised a strategy to remove the residents of New York City from danger and relocate us to safety?"

Blum's neutral facade cracked a small grin as he imagined his rifle's stock glancing off the bridge of her surgically-altered nose. "Our resupply is scheduled for EOD today. We're working through the logistics of a full evacuation as we speak. Now, for your safety and mine, please return to your apartment's interior and lock your doors. Remain in place until we notify you it's safe to retrieve your rations."

"Retrieve? I feel unsafe exiting the confines of my *penthouse.* I'll require them to be delivered and stowed appropriately."

Blum's body vibrated against the urge to throttle the socialite. "Get back in your *apartment.* Doing so will enable me and my soldiers to continue guarding the perimeter. We do this to ensure you, and the tens of thousands of people sheltering in Central Park, avoid being eaten... alive. Good day."

Blum nodded as the elevator doors closed on Pamela's shrieking demands to *hold court* with his superior officer. "Maybe saving humanity isn't our best option, at least not *all* of it," he mused as the elevator bounced softly on the ground floor.

Blum's head snapped toward the entrance as his boots hit the lobby's marble tiles. Gunfire competed with desperate screams as his men retreated from the Grand Army Plaza gate.

"What the? Sapano, SITREP!" he yelled into his boom mic as he rushed from the building toward his soldier's rapidly deteriorating skirmish line.

"We've been overrun."

"Pull back to the Park Road barricade. Do not let them enter the park!"

Blum exploded into the fray, sweeping his M4 right to left, mangling the legs of the infected marching toward his men. "Blum for command. Our position has been breached. Send backup A-SAP! Repeat, we have been breached. Redirect every available gun to the GAP gate."

A thump deep in his chest told him air support was en route. "Sapano, Black Hawks closing fast. Hold the line."

Sapano didn't acknowledge.

"Sapano!" static filled Blum's earpiece.

Blum swapped magazines and laid down another string of fire. He couldn't allow the infected to reach the refugee camps; the unarmed, wholly unprotected civilians would be slaughtered. But the overwhelming numbers of infected rampaging through the streets guaranteed he'd be forced to watch a mass casualty event unfold.

A guttural scream spun Blum on his heel. A tall, wiry man had pinned a young woman against the barrier, his mouth latched to her neck. Life faded from her eyes as her attacker tugged on her flesh.

“You rotten son of a bitch,” Blum shouted, as he shouldered his rifle.

The infected man pivoted to face Blum. Through his rifle’s optics, he noticed something different. Although black as pitch, his eyes held an intelligence Blum hadn’t witnessed in other infected. He froze. Was this one human enough to save? His indecision ended when the monster’s head flipped back, swallowing a ragged hunk of flesh.

Refocused, Blum took the shot just as a tattered body blundered in front of his target, absorbing the bullet with her chest. When she dropped from sight, the man had vanished.

The purr of a Black Hawk’s minigun flooded him with hope. He followed the tracer rounds to a rocky outcropping and pulled a sharp breath as his headset buzzed with panicked voices. The Hawk’s gunner wasn’t there to reinforce his besieged team, but to scorch the earth. The Hawk’s rocket pods flared, providing grim confirmation that they’d been forsaken and their blood would spill with that of the infected.

Shaking off his daze, Blum scrambled for the building he’d just left. If he could secure an elevated position, maybe, just maybe, he could sufficiently thin the infected and end the slaughter.

***

Blum slapped the elevator lockout button as he exited on the seventeenth floor and hard stepped to the private entrance. The floor's only inhabitant, the bane of his existence, didn't know he was coming. After two swift kicks, and an inflexible slam of his shoulder, the door lost its battle to remain sealed.

Blum ignored Pamela Wentworth's shrieked protest and marched to the expansive apartment's wraparound balcony overlooking Central Park and the GAP gate. The sky was thick with Black Hawk gunships and Apache attack helicopters. They hovered to fire upon the humanity below, then slid left and right, performing an aerial ballet of death and destruction.

Blum understood instantly what had happened. New York City had fallen.

Chapter 30

Seated in an uncomfortable metal folding chair under the early morning sun, Abe pinched the bridge of his nose, convinced if another person complained about some mundane, trivial issue, he'd throttle them all. From the corner of his eye, he noticed Ann fidgeting in her chair. When their eyes met, a message passed between them. *They're all idiots.*

Abe recognized the significance of his and Ann's concurrence. It marked the second time during the roadside neighborhood meeting it happened. Considering the prior evening's *disagreement*, Abe had expected her to spit nails into his forehead when he arrived. Instead, she simply nodded and winked. He'd sic Lu on her later to flush out the cause of her sudden change of heart.

"Who's going to maintain the property surrounding the fence?" the chunky pseudo-intellectual running the meeting asked, glaring authoritatively over the rim of his glasses.

"Are you shitting me?" the words escaped Abe's mouth before his mind registered it had hinged open. "Have you watched the news? Any of you? We're dealing with an extinction level event because, you know, people are dying, reanimating, and eating the living. They literally strip flesh from bone, put it in their mouths, and swallow. And so far I've heard you morons gripe about mail delivery challenges posed by the fence, road repairs, and now who'll do, what, edge along the fence?"

"Abel, please raise your hand and request permission to speak. We must maintain civility in order to avoid societal collapse."

Abe's brow crooked. He didn't recognize the man scolding him and was unsure how the pompous buffoon knew his name. But he'd had enough.

"Society already collapsed — whoever you are. It collapsed so hard the ground shook. But I suppose you were too preoccupied with tending a rose garden or pontificating how our fence may interfere with the migration habits of geese to notice. Why are you even running this meeting? From the looks of it, the only physical work you've done is flipping through the pages of Plato's Symposium, which you don't understand, but assume it makes you look intelligent. I move to have Ann run the meeting so we might actually get to the business of survival before nightfall!"

The eyes of his neighbors fell on him, and Lu's grip tightened on his leg as the silence after his outburst dragged on. "I second the motion," Randy said from between Bina and Ann.

Soon, the entire gathering had supported Abe's nomination of Ann.

"Stanley."

"What?" Abe snipped at the man.

"My name is Stanley, and I meant no disrespect. However, I'd be remiss to allow the actions of a hotheaded Neanderthal to subvert my well-intentioned suggestions sans an explanation. Life's tiny normalities allow one to maintain a sense of security in an environment that is anything but secure. We must establish a work distribution schedule allowing, dare I say, encouraging each of us to engage with our surroundings, our neighbors, our *very souls*."

"Our *very souls,"* Abe mocked, matching Stanley's dramatic delivery. "Ann, for the love of sweet baby Jesus, take the reins before I have an aneurism and my *hot head* explodes."

On her way to the front of the gathering, Ann cocked an eyebrow and mouthed, *Plato's Symposium*? To which Abe simply shrugged.

"Stan, move. Go sit with your wife," Ann ordered in response to Stanley's hesitation to surrender control of the meeting.

"My word!"

"We've been listening to *your word* for over an hour. And, I'm sure everyone will agree we feel dumber. So, *please* move." Ann's tone held her customary edge, which Abe had assumed she reserved for him and Randy, and was the reason he'd nominated her.

Ann got to the business of survival when she faced her neighbors. "You may have noticed seven households missing this morning. I contacted each last night. All confirmed they would attend and denied being bitten, scratched, or otherwise affected by whatever it is causing this..." Her words trailed, unable to speak the truth about what was happening.

"I called all of you this morning, reminding you about this meeting. Those seven households failed to answer my calls. We cannot permit this illness to breach our fence line." Ann paused, allowing her inference to churn through the gathering.

"I'm asking for volunteers to investigate those homes."

Abe met Randy's stare and nodded in confirmation of both the assumption they'd made yesterday and that they were willing to clear those homes.

"I see we have two volunteers. Others?"

"I'm in," a man Abe found vaguely familiar offered.

"Thank you, Gage. Anyone else?"

"Next point of business," Ann began after a lengthy pause, "we need people guarding our gates and on foot patrol. With only three streets and eighty-four households in our little community, I don't believe gate guards will see much, if any, traffic, especially over the next several days."

"Ann," Abe interjected, "I'd like to address the group."

Lu's grip on Abe's leg tightened to vice-like and Ann's chin sank to her chest. "Hey, everyone, relax. I've got notes so I'll stay on topic. You may not like my topics, but you should listen."

Ann stepped to the side, a movement meant to surrender the floor to Abe.

"Alright, listen up, here's the brass tacks. Volunteer or Stan-the-Man will start assigning grounds keeping duties. We're responsible for our own safety. The military's on its heels. With what happened in New York yesterday, they'll resort to a shoot-first posture. Meaning, if we don't keep our fence from being breached, and they catch wind of our struggles, they're going to send those same Black Hawks from New York to visit us. Ann will create a list of roles that need to be filled. I'll circulate it to each of you. Sign up for something, preferably something you're familiar doing. Also, be prepared to donate two cans of food, boxed foods are acceptable. We'll call it a pantry, and I don't care who's put in charge of it, as long as we have one. You'll thank me later."

Abe glanced around the crowd. He recognized some of them and was certain he didn't like any of them. "Also, for those of you who attacked my home yesterday, I'll be accepting apologies and thank yous this evening between the hours..."

"Okay, Abe. I'll take it from here," Ann interrupted, dismissing him as she retook control of the meeting.

***

"I was hoping she'd let you keep talking," Nic bellowed in her patented gregarious style. "You were warming up for a classic rant!"

Abe ignored her and remained focused on his gear. His kit needed to be squared away before he met Randy at the Albertson house, the first on their list to clear. He didn't know this Gage guy either, and wanted to at least get a read on him before busting into a house with him.

"Did you really want everyone to thank you and apologize?"

"Stop speaking, Nic. Aren't you supposed to be guarding the gate?"

"I'm on foot patrol. Keeping the streets safe, so watch yourself. My shift starts tomorrow morning."

"Where's Lu?"

"Still mad at you for volunteering to clear houses."

"Not what I asked."

"She's with Ann. I think they're developing a leadership structure. And — she's still mad at you."

"Alright, I'll touch base with her on my way to Randy's. While I'm gone, make yourself useful and inventory our food. To be clear, inventory, don't *consume.* And don't touch my guns... I'll know if you did."

"What if I lick them?"

Abe recoiled at the visual then smirked. "Let me know how cleaning solvent and gun oil tastes. You, uh, uh, seem to have recovered nicely from your trauma. Maybe you should move back home. I hear Westlake is holding up quite well. You'll be safe."

Nic's eyes narrowed as she walked slowly away from the front door. "Lu said I can stay as long as I like. And so did you! I'd like to stay until this ends."

"So, forever, that's what you're saying. You'll live here forever? I find that prospect untenable."

"If you lived through my *trauma*, you'd understand," Nic's voice was strained and she kept inching away from the door in case Abe tried to bum-rush her from the house.

"I thought you were always bringing smoke and throwing hands? What happened to tough-chick-Nic? Couple zombies jump in your face and you folded like origami... sad."

"Oh, I can throw some hands. Keep talking and I'll show you how many hands I throw when I'm throwing hands." Nic winced at her feeble comeback.

"Two, Nic. You'll always just throw two hands — still sad. I'm leaving. Make yourself useful and keep your grubby paws off my guns."

It surprised Abe to find Lu seated in her favorite Adirondack on their front porch. Her head rested heavily against the chair's high back, her eyes focused on something unseen in their front yard.

"Hey, I thought you were with Ann?"

"We should be doing yard work. Planting flowers and cutting grass. Instead, you're about to go fight monsters that used to be our neighbors."

Abe recognized Lu's tenor; her misty eyes never left the yard as Abe sat next to her. "I know, babe. But here we are and we have to focus on survival. That means you go work with Ann, Nic guards the streets, and I go clear a couple of houses. We keep doing that. Next thing you know, we'll be expanding the fence line, growing our numbers, and rebuilding. Just stay focused on living. It all restarts today. We're the future. We'll make it bright, I promise."

"You impress me sometimes, Abel Willings, when you suddenly become human. It never lasts, but it's nice when it happens."

"I'm nice like that. Plus, look at it this way. We never have to cut grass again!"

"I hope you're wrong."

Abe held Lu's hand and joined her in remembering better times. "Babe, I gotta go. Randy's waiting," he said softly, breaking their reverie.

"I know. Please be careful."

Abe leaned into Lu and touched his forehead to hers. "Always."

Chapter 31

Even after hours spent assembling his kit, Abe patted every pocket in his tactical ensemble for the third time as he rounded the corner. He hoped he packed everything he'd need. But when he set eyes on Randy, he realized it wouldn't matter if he forgot something, because Randy had apparently brought every battle implement he owned.

Abe's pace quickened as Randy and Gage stood at the edge of the Albertson's front yard. Any other day, it would have appeared that neighbors were engaging in a friendly conversation about fertilizers or scheming ways to stop the mailman from cutting across their yards. But it wasn't any other day. It was day two of the apocalypse.

"'Bout time," Randy said when Abe joined them. "We were thinking maybe you bailed on us."

"Nah, had some wife issues to deal with."

"Ain't that the truth," Gage said as a knowing look flashed across his features.

"I'm Abe," he said, offering Gage his hand.

"Um, Abe. I know, I live two doors from you. We had beers together during the block party last summer."

"I got nothing."

"You said you liked my car — the corvette. Our wives walk together every day, after work."

"So, tell me, Gage," Abe said, changing the subject, "can you shoot? I see guns, but do you know how to use them? I don't want to get shot by some weekend warrior."

"Gage is ex-military," Randy interjected.

"That doesn't answer my question. He could have been a sanitation specialist or clerical specialist."

"I was infantry, two deployments to Iraq. I can shoot," Gage answered flatly.

"Okay, but I'm still watching you. So, who's on point?"

"Whoa, how about we develop a plan before we go blasting into a potentially dangerous situation?"

"He's got a point, Abe."

Abe nodded to Gage, a silent request to share his plan. "The Albertson's home is the same style as mine. The basement is all home mechanics, so we'll enter through the lower level. Randy will breach. I'm on point. Upon entry, Abe covers our left flank, Randy our right. We clear the basement and move to the main floor. We'll exit the basement directly into the kitchen, clear it and move to the living room, then the second level. Stay a minimum of an arm's length from one another. We get bunched up — the enemy makes quick work of us. If we encounter a locked door, we breach it — same as the basement. Watch your lines of fire, call out reloads or malfunctions, and keep your head on a swivel. We're searching for three targets. Clear?"

"Clear! Let's move before I change my mind," Randy said.

Abe's head pivoted between Randy and Gage. A fuzzy memory nibbling at his skull threw him off kilter. "Clear," he finally croaked, stuffing his apprehension.

Gage nodded stiffly. "Alright, let's roll."

Chapter 32

"On three," Gage said.

"On three," Randy confirmed then slammed his foot against the door, shattering the lock.

"I think he gets too excited," Abe said, answering Gage's questioning gaze.

Gage shook off his bewilderment and entered the basement with his rifle tucked tight against his shoulder. Weapon lights flared through the gloom, casting shadows throughout the undisturbed cavernous area. Its tranquility belied the unspoken fate of its inhabitants.

"Clear," Gage whispered. "Move to the second floor."

A floorboard rattling thump sent the trio's rifles skyward. "Well, they're home," Gage said quietly. "If the door's unlocked, we enter quietly and engage on contact. If it's locked, we send three rounds through, then breach."

"Wait," Randy began, "is this actual engaging or the other engaging?"

"What?" Gage asked, his features knotted with confusion.

"Bait," Abe answered. "He associates engaging with being used as bait. Long story."

"Actual engaging."

"Got it. Lead on, good sir," Randy quipped.

As they reached the tight landing, the stench wafting around the gaps of the closed door leading to the kitchen forced a step back.

"Holy hell," Randy said, covering his nose with the back of his hand. "Smells like some kid's science experiment went horribly wrong."

Abe shushed his friend, and strained to hear any signs of movement. Silence. Their forced entry had been wildly loud, the stair treads had squeaked beneath their boots during their ascent, and they'd abandoned whispered communications, so they should hear the monsters shuffling through the house preparing for the food to deliver itself. But it was pin-drop quiet.

Randy moved into position and prepared to breach when Abe's nibble turned into a jolting bite. They can think past simply searching for food by planning and scheming to trick it into coming to them. He'd watched it happen on the highway, and heard the story Finn told about the parking garage. *They're waiting for us!*

"It's a trap!"

Abe's words stopped Randy's foot mid-flight. The sudden action tossed Randy off balance and sent him twisting to the ground with a deep, resonating thud.

"What the h..." Abe covered Randy's mouth, cutting his angry rant short, then put his ear against the door and waited.

"Yep, I hear their rasping. They've set up an ambush," Abe whispered. "Randy, you're with me. Gage, you hold this position. After you hear us breach the front door. Count to ten and hard step into the kitchen. We'll catch them in a crossfire."

***

"Okay, kick it on my command."

"What, no three count?" Randy asked earnestly.

Abe's eyes bulged, and he shoved his friend toward the door by the shoulder. "Kick the damn door, Randy!"

Randy's size-thirteen stomper slammed against the door, then again, winning the battle on his third try. The door swung open violently, bounced off the wall, and shot back at them as they rushed into the house with their weapons at high ready. The noxious odor they'd smelled in the basement was overwhelming on the main floor, eliciting muffled gags.

When nothing attacked, Abe whipped at his watering eyes and started a silent ten count; he realized the infected were still waiting by the basement door. When Gage breached, they'd overpower him in a flash.

"Move. Kitchen. Now!" Abe barked, taking point and rushing to disrupt the ambush waiting for Gage.

Abe cut through the expansive living room in a blaze and burst into the kitchen as his internal countdown stroked ten. He found two targets kneeling on either side of the basement door. "Randy, watch your back. One of them has gone rogue."

Randy spun as the basement door exploded from its frame and Abe ended the closest infected with a round to the back of its skull, splattering red tinted white fluff in every direction. Gage backpedaled onto the landing, startled by the rifle's report, narrowly evading the second lurching monster's grasp.

Abe turned sharply as Randy's startled yelp rose above the ringing in his ears. His friend was locked in mortal combat with their third target, and losing the fight. The Z's grip on Randy's tactical vest was unyielding as gnashing teeth darted at his friend's flesh. Randy struggled to fend off the attacks by wedging his AR between them. His muscular arms displayed a roadmap of swelling veins as he pushed against the beast with all of his strength.

"Little help," Randy screeched.

Abe accelerated toward the fray, unsheathed his blade, and thrust it through the monster's cranium.

"You son of a bitch!" Gage howled, spinning Abe on his heel to discover the ex-military operator struggling to evade their final target's snapping jaws. The man's corded forearm bulged as his grip tightened around the monster's neck to little effect.

"Destroy its brain!" Abe shouted as he ripped his K-Bar free of his kill's splintered skull.

"I can't let go," Gage answered as the zombie thrashed against his grasp.

Abe bounded over the unmoving body of the first infected he'd killed. His knee pads clacked against tile as he landed and plunged his blade through the monster's eye.

"Abe, that part about destroying its brain," Gage yelled, as he scrambled to avoid the goo leaking from the Z's eye, "falls under the heading of something you should've told me fifteen minutes ago!"

"Have you ever watched a zombie movie? Everyone knows it's all about headshots! Plus, I thought you military guys were ready for anything."

"Un-wad your panties and stop your bickering. I heard something upstairs," Randy interrupted.

"Are you kidding me? I thought we only had three targets!"

A thump similar to the one they'd heard in the basement followed instantly by a door rattling in its frame hushed the trio. "Gage, take it up with Ann. Tell her she can't count. Let me know how it works out for you," Abe mumbled as he slid into position a few yards from the enclosed staircase. "Randy, go right. Gage, you go left. If I run, start shooting."

"That's a terrible plan."

"He has a lot of them, Gage. But he won't listen to reason, so save your breath."

"Let me know when you're done whining, but make it quick. We have six more houses to clear."

Randy kneeled next to the staircase opening and nodded. Abe glanced to Gage and received a thumb up. "If you're not dead, come down with your hands above your head!"

"If you're not dead?" Randy mouthed.

"Don't shoot me," a small voice squeaked from the second floor shadows. "I just want to go home."

"Show yourself with your hands over your head."

Frightened, red-rimmed eyes stared at Abe from behind a tangle of mousy hair. "What's your name, sweetheart?" Abe asked gently.

"Lynn, my name is Lynn. Wh... What's happening to everyone? Mister Albertson attacked Vicky and her mom, then they all came after me," she sobbed. "He bit Vicky's nose off and, and he ate it. I want to go *home.*"

"Put your arms down. Lynn, kiddo, how old are you?"

"I'm fourteen," she answered, wiping tears from her cheeks. "Can I get my phone and call my mom?"

"Come down, and we'll work on getting you home. But, before we do, were you bitten or scratched?"

"No," Lynn answered through a quivering bottom lip. "I ran up here as soon as they all went crazy."

"Why were you here?" Abe asked as unsteady legs carried Lynn down the stairs, and Randy and Gage repositioned behind him.

"My mom asked Vicky's mom to watch me while she tried to get out of work. They sent us home early from school because of some emergency."

Abe scanned her, focusing on her neck and arms. He didn't see any noticeable signs of trauma, but understood she'd have to be checked closer. "Where's your phone?"

"I don't know, I threw it at Vicky after she, um, she..."

"Tell ya what, kiddo. Have a seat and we'll look for it. But you have to promise you'll stay put. Deal?"

"Is this it?" Randy chirped, waving a sleek black cell phone back and forth.

Lynn nodded, as gasping sobs stole her breath, and she took the phone from Randy.

Abe bobbed his head, indicating to Randy and Gage to join him out of Lynn's earshot. "We have to check her for bites. I didn't see any obvious marks, but we've got to make sure."

They fell silent, each mulling through what that meant and how, exactly, a fourteen-year-old girl would react when three grown men told her they'd need to inspect her for bites. "I'll call Bina," Randy finally offered.

"Oh, thank God!" Abe blurted.

***

"Come with me, sweetheart," Bina said with motherly charm. "These big, powerful men are afraid of you. They need me to make sure you're not hurt."

"My mom isn't answering her phone," Lynn said, just above a whisper. "I want to go home, but she's not answering."

"Don't you fret; we'll get a hold of her. The cell lines have been pretty sketchy. You can stay with us until we get through to your mom."

Bina glanced knowingly at the trio as she put her arm around Lynn and led her to the door. Her eyes suddenly filled with sadness and conveyed a solemn message. Lynn was their community's first refugee.

Chapter 33

"I'm not calling him — he told me it wouldn't work and I swear I'll shoot him if I have to listen to him gloat for days on end."

"Stone Willings! Your plan didn't fail. You can't help that Patty lied. How were you supposed to know she smuggled her infected sister into our compound in her trunk!"

Stone, perched in his second-story window, sent three rounds of 6.5 Creedmoor through the skulls of an equal number of zombies stumbling up his lawn. "I'm not calling. We'll be fine. We've got plenty of food, guns, and ammo. I promise we'll make it. Show a little faith in your husband!"

Kat checked her phone for a signal then slipped from the room as Stone mumbled something about 'that white stuff being nasty.'

"Lu, don't talk, just listen," Kat whispered. "Some idiot brought the infection to our doorstep. But Stone's too damn bullheaded to ask Abe for help. Can you have him call Stone? Don't tell him why. Say Stone needs to ask a question... something about a gun malfunctioning. Can you do that?"

"Kat, honey, Abe's asleep. He was out clearing houses until early this morning. I'll wake him and tell him to call, but I'm warning you, he's going to be in a foul mood."

"When isn't Abe in a foul mood?"

"Good point. Give me ten... Kat, how bad is it?"

"Bad — terrible, actually. The infection swarmed through our neighborhood like bees on honey. Stone's just heartbroken his defenses failed. He's been in a daze, mumbling nonsense about the apocalypse not going as planned. Did you know our husbands planned for this shit?"

Lu chewed her bottom lip. She had known, but wrote it off to them being unbalanced, zombie movie watching, gun nuts. "I kinda did. Didn't you?"

"I thought they were planning for some other disaster, like financial collapse or tornados. But zombies, Lu... flipping zombies!"

Gunfire in the background snapped them back on topic. "Just have Abe call. We need to get out of here."

"Give me ten. And, Kat, please be careful."

***

"Yo, big dog, how's day three of the apocalypse treating you?" Abe asked wearily, while sipping a cup of coffee. "My apocalypse is proving far more complicated than I imagined. Wait till I tell you what I've been up to. But, you first."

"'Bout the same as you," Stone answered, his breaths heavy and labored. "Sorry I haven't radioed. Got um, sidetracked. Look, Abe, I'm kinda in the middle of something. Can I call you back?"

"Oh, sorry. Lu told me you called and wanted to talk. Said you had an AR malfunctioning?"

The brothers sat quietly as reality churned. "Damn Kat!"

"What's going on, Stone?"

"Nothing I can't handle. Just a minor outbreak caused by a moron named Patty."

"Let me guess, she got past your inspections, either before they started or hid it from you?"

"How'd you know?"

"I just cleared seven houses with the same issue. Can't say I blame them for trying, but now we have cleaning crews scrap-ing chunks of skulls and body parts off walls. I'm just thankful they didn't escape onto our streets."

Abe sensed Stone's internal debate. "Do you need help, Stone?"

"I'll be good... well, maybe a little help wouldn't hurt. But, we have some issues. The shipping container gates are locked and ringed in razor-wire. And, if you do bust through them, we've got at least twenty Zs stumbling around. I'm thinning them, but more keep popping up."

"How about that nasty white crap they spew when you bust their melons?"

"Hold on!" Stone shouted then let loose a mini-barrage. "Yeah, I could use some help, no maybes about it."

"Hold tight. I'll round up Randy. Give us about an hour. Stage your supplies by the back door. We'll bring a few trucks and SUVs. Be ready."

"*Whoa*, I'm not evacuating. This is my home. I'm not going to, to, surrender it to these monsters. Not a chance, Abe, not a flipping chance!"

"Stone, I understand how you feel. But if I remember your plans, you have about thirty homes behind your barriers. We can't clear thirty homes, brother. We simply can't. You're better off relocating here until we put together a plan to retake your neighborhood."

Abe understood what was happening. Stone, the smartest person he knew, was struggling to admit defeat. He couldn't fault him. Abe had busted his chops for years about his shipping container strategy, but never told Stone it was because it was a better plan than his fence. But only because of the compact layout of Stone's neighborhood. It was a good time to come clean and boost his brother's ego. A good brother would do that. Too bad Abe was his brother.

"Abel, I want to sleep in my own bed, in my own house, in my own neighborhood. I'm not relocating."

Abe's jaw hinged open, then clamped as Kat's piercing rant filtered through. "I'm going to relocate. You... you can stay here and get eaten alive if you want. Abe, come get me. Your brother can fend for himself."

“Stone, hang tight. I’m on my way.”

Abe set his phone on the kitchen table, swished some coffee through his teeth, and stretched. His body wasn’t what it once was, and protested every second of yesterday’s action. He hadn’t counted on it rolling into today’s early morning hours. But he was going to eat some bacon and eggs after he helped his brother. Cholesterol be damned!

Snickers and whispers focused his attention across the table. “What?”

“You look old!” Nic quipped. “Your hair's a mess, you have bags under your eyes, and every joint in your body just popped during that Gawd-awful stretch. You sure you’re up to playing Captain America today?”

“Lu, your friend has overstayed her welcome. She needs to go home,” Abe said, never breaking his contemptuous glare with Nic.

“Well, we have seven vacant houses, so maybe I’ll work with Ann on getting Nic her own place.”

“Not the ones by the gates!” Abe practically shouted. “We’ll need those for quarantine. I was going to talk to Ann about it. But, since you volunteered...” Abe trailed off when he turned to face Lu and found her donning the tactical vest he’d bought her as an anniversary gift years earlier.

“What?”

"Why are you dressed like that?" he asked suspiciously. "I thought you were working with Ann?"

"I am — right after we rescue your brother and Kat."

"Nope! Not going to happen."

"I'm going, too," Nic chimed.

"See, now you're just trying to make me mad," Abe said, running a hand down his face.

"We're going, Abe. So sack up and roll your ass!"

"Lu, I forbid it. You have been FORBADE!"

Chapter 34

"This is bullshit!" Abe hollered as Lu bumped her Tahoe over a tree lawn to avoid a tangled mess of steel blocking their path.

They were an hour into what should have taken ten minutes. Main roads and side streets had transformed into parking lots and, sometimes, battlefields, slowing their travel to a crawl.

Yet, amidst the carnage, Abe noticed people still scrambling to fortify their homes as Lu traversed the debris-littered pavement. He couldn't decide if their display was inspiring for its defiance or simply a futile last gasp to survive. Either way, he knew they were too late, their fate sealed by inaction fostered by a misguided trust that an overwhelmed military would quell the infected.

He'd also noticed, in a few areas, where bottlenecks created by abandoned cars were seemingly cleared by heavy equipment. The results formed a manmade barrier separating front yards from streets with tons of steel and rubber. A strategy he aimed to adopt.

"Man, oh, man, you complain a lot! Seriously, Abe, if you didn't complain, you'd literally never talk!"

"Nic, weren't you supposed to start your street patrol today? You know, like a *streetwalker*!"

"*Like a streetwalker,*" Nic mimicked, her tenor pitched. "I'm on early shift, guarding you while you sleep. Oh, by the way, *Ann* asked me to lead the team."

"I find the prospect of you traipsing around with a loaded gun mere feet from my house disturbing! The fact you'll be leading others, also with loaded weapons, is terrifying."

"Holy..." Lu mumbled, hitting the brakes and nearly causing Randy's F250 to rear-end them.

"What the hell's going on here?" Abe chimed, taking in the scene.

A miles long sea of brake lights weaved a glowing trail to a supercenter's parking lot, and it wasn't moving. Abe scanned the immediate area, searching for a clear path to any side streets offering an escape from the gridlock. Reaching into his backpack, he hauled out his Bushnell binoculars, tapped the sunroof's *open* button, and shimmied through.

"What a mess," he exclaimed.

A large military force had fenced in the parking lot and cordoned off the entrance, restricting access until they completed a quick inspection of a vehicle's inhabitants, then waved them into a single file line. He couldn't see the storefront, but the number of idling vehicles waiting their turn painted a picture of absolute chaos.

Military foot patrols marched the length of the traffic jam, their heads swiveling left to right. Abe knew they'd be the first to fall when the infected launched their attack. And they *would* attack.

"Lu, take the sidewalk, then cut into the gas station. We should be able to force our way through the hedgerow onto Lakeview and take it to Riverview. It'll be a straight shot to Stone's house from there."

Abe radioed their plan to Randy and Gage as Lu bounced her SUV over the curb and trounced on the accelerator, forcing Abe to retreat from the sunroof and brace for impact.

"Hold on," Lu whooped as the hedgerow raced toward them.

Abe floated from his seat, then slammed back down as the SUV landed roughly on Lakeview, cut right, and sped toward Riverview.

***

"Are any of your neighbors still... alive?"

"Abe, I don't know. Kat hasn't been able to raise any of them via cell or radio. But I can't guarantee they're not hunkered in a crawlspace or attic and not getting a signal."

Abe walked the gate's length, probing for weak spots. The shipping container serving as the community's rear entry point was locked from the inside. The fence to either side glistened with razor wire. At the fence's inner base, large chunks of concrete ringed with caltrops awaited anyone foolish enough to scale its six feet and free-drop to the ground. His brother had indeed been diligent in shoring up his defensive perimeter.

“Why’d you ask about my neighbors?”

“Well, Stone, it’s like this. You’re, no matter what you think, leaving here today. And when we leave, this gate is getting locked from the outside. Hopefully, anyone still alive will see what’s happening and break for the exit while it’s open.”

Abe waited for Stone’s reply. Most of the time, his brother was a rational guy, a deep thinker. But this was his home and Abe was forcing him to abandon it and admit defeat — a jagged pill for any man to swallow.

“Okay, what’s the plan?” Stone asked, with pained resignation.

“Well, I believe this will prove one of my better strategies.”

“Terrible plan, Abe, just terrible!” Randy yelled as he crawled along the heavy wooden plank he and Gage laid over the razor wire strung across the top of the shipping container.

“Actually, it’s a brilliant plan. You’re just an uncoordinated mutt with crappy balance. If you’d stop talking and concentrate, you’d already be on the other side.”

Randy froze as he reached the plank's end, took a deep breath, then carefully crawled to the open space between the razor wire and container’s edge. His eyes blurred with stinging sweat; he swiped at the moisture leaking from his forehead as he cautiously maneuvered to his feet, desperately trying to avoid tumbling over the edge and into the infected mob below.

Gage watched Randy go wobbly then slam to his knees. *This isn't going to end well.*

"I'm not good with heights. I need some help."

"Help? How the hell am I supposed to help you with that?"

"Suck it up, Randy," Abe yelled from the bed of his friend's truck, "you'll be on the ground in a couple. We don't have time for your drama!"

"Abe, we've got a problem," Gage called over his shoulder.

"He passed out, didn't he?"

"Like a drunk on a bender. He probably dinged his noggin. He went down hard."

Abe rubbed his temples. He knew this would happen, but Randy insisted the container was low enough that it wouldn't trigger his fear of heights. "Lu, you and Nic have our six. Shoot anyone or anything that looks sketchy or even has a runny nose."

"What's our *six*?"

"Do you ever listen to me? Don't answer. You're guarding our backs, our rear flank, our blind-approach. Clear?"

"Clear!"

"If I were you, I'd leave Nic at street level while you take the high position in the truck bed. She'll be fine."

"Abe, getting a little hot."

"On my way," Abe said, hoisting himself to the top of the container from the bed of Randy's truck and rushing to join Gage.

The space between the razor wire and the container's edge was tight, much tighter than he'd thought when viewing it from the ground. With Randy sprawled out and Gage covering their right flank, Abe took up their left flank, slightly behind his slumbering friend.

The street below was jammed tight with infected, each vying for a position directly below them, their mouths working furiously to latch onto the meat ten feet above. The scene reminded Abe of a school of carp fighting for a crust of bread.

"Stone," Abe shouted into his radio, "I thought you said twenty of these things were roaming around?"

"No, I said *at least twenty,* then I said *they keep popping up*. I'll try to be more accurate with my census collection next time."

"Nobody I know can count," Abe mumbled while scowling at his radio. "Can you thin their rear edge?"

"Negative, I'm unlocking the front gate, like *your plan* dictated. Kat is pulling our supplies together. You'll have to hit them head on."

Abe glanced down at Randy. A rivulet of drool streaming from his mouth had puddled under his face. "Gage," he said, "it's just you and me. Time to make the doughnuts!"

Gage opened fire, cutting through the horde with disciplined, flawlessly placed shots, dropping a Z with each stroke of his AR's trigger. Abe inched left and brought his rifle online with considerably less discipline than his counterpart.

Abe's plan was simple; clear the area of infected, drop to the ground, snap the gate's lock, and let Lu and Nic roll in. They'd rally at Stone's, load up his supplies, and evacuate through the front gate. But Stone appeared to have underestimated the Zs by an order of magnitude. Plus, their gunfire was sure to draw infected from the surrounding community, leaving Lu and Nic exposed and woefully ill-equipped to fend off a full-scale assault.

Abe's shots increased in time with his thumping heart, resulting in an abysmal kill ratio. They had to get the gate opened A-SAP.

"Abe," Gage yelled over the din, "concentrate on the ones against the container. I'll thin them from the rear."

Abe bit back his retort. Gage was right. He was wasting time and ammo. He swallowed his pride and inched forward as far as Randy's prone body would allow and adjusted his fire. But Randy's unmoving form prevented him from reaching the container's edge.

"Wake-up," he shouted, shaking Randy's shoulder. "Wake-up, wake-up, wake-up! You're in my way."

Randy startled to consciousness, his angry scowl locked onto Abe. "What the hell are you doing in my bedroom?" he asked, dragging the back of his hand across his mouth.

"No time to explain. Get out of my way!"

Randy flinched as hot brass from Abe's AR pinged off his forehead, clearing his senses and reminding him where he was and what had happened. "You should have tried harder to stop me from coming up here. You know I'm bad with heights."

"I'll kick you right over the side, Randy. I'm not kidding, over the side! Go help Lu and Nic, and don't look down. You're too damn big to carry!"

Abe slid into the space vacated by Randy and knelt at the very edge of the container, then unleashed a stream of copper-jacketed death. He soon realized kneeling on both knees was a recipe for disaster as he tipped forward, nearly tumbling into the open maws below.

When his AR's bolt locked back, Abe moved to swap magazines, adjust his firing stance, and let the empty mag fall free. Eyeing the lip of the container as a brace, he swung his left leg toward his target, dragged his heel through Randy's drool puddle, and watched in morbid fascination as his booted-foot slipped from the container. His right leg buckled as his body instinctively rocked back to keep from following his leg's trajectory, threatening to drop him into the razor-wire jungle inches away.

Without thought, Abe over-corrected off his right leg and succeeded in catapulting himself from the shipping container. His belly-flop-landing atop the savagely active infected, toppled a large swath of them to the pavement. Scrambling to his knees, he swung his head around, searching for a path to safety.

"RUN!" Gage yelled.

Abe sprang from the pile of undulating bodies and set course for the safety of Stone's house, shaking free of grasping, infected hands as he bolted through a quickly collapsing sliver in the zombie phalanx. "Stone, hide. I'm coming in hot and bringing company!"

"I know — you're running right at me. Break right, I'll cover your retreat."

Abe zigged hard to the right and pushed through waist-high shrubs when Stone's Tavor barked to life. "Hey, Abe, you're *engaging* like a pro, but you may want to throw your gun in the mix."

Abe grimaced at Randy's dual jab and slammed to a stop, turned, and entered the fight. Gage crushed the horde from the rear while Stone blasted away at the leading edge. Again, Abe noticed they moved faster than he'd expected, but were by no means fleet of foot, and couldn't escape the blistering cross fire they'd stumbled into.

Abe's red dot bounced rapidly, trying to line up head shots, but it was futile, so he shifted aim to their legs and hips, crippling dozens in a matter of seconds.

"Stone," Abe radioed, "relock the front gate and rally at the rear gate. Tell Randy and Lu to hightail it to your house. I'll finish the infected. We're losing light, MOVE!"

Gage joined Abe as he worked his way from the edge of the downed zombies, putting a round through every head, careful to avoid the fluff and other vile fluids leaking from their ravaged bodies.

"Abe, we've loaded what we can, but a lot of supplies are getting left behind. Valuable supplies!"

"I'll be there in a second," Abe radioed back. "Stone, we'll come back for the rest. Lock up your house and let's get the hell outta here!"

Abe stood silent as Stone secured the last of several locks, sealing off his neighborhood from the outside world. His brother's hand trembled as he stroked the cold steel container. His home had been overrun, yanked from his grasp and claimed by the dead. It was painful to watch.

"STONE, on your right!" Gage yelled, angling left for a better line of fire.

When Stone spun, he came face to gnashing maw with a gruesomely damaged infected and sent his gloved right hand arching for the monster's jaw, shattering it on impact.

"Should we stop him?" Randy asked as Stone kicked and stomped the downed zombie, his string of obscenities growing in volume with each blow.

"Nah, let him have this. We'll corral him in a couple."

Chapter 35

Sergeant Finn backpedaled, twisted right, and plunged his K-Bar deep into the temple of an infected who'd broken through their line. "Aim for their legs!"

His order dropped his soldier's muzzles by six inches and focused them on slowing the shambling mob's advance. They were less than ten yards away, with only muck-slicked pavement separating them.

It was only a bandage. If they didn't find cover A-SAP, they'd be overrun and shredded. As the infected he'd just killed dropped, and his knife freed with a wet slurp, Finn scanned his team. He was down to four sets of boots after losing Spangler, Sanders, and Comer to the rampaging abominations.

"Billings, break off and find us a hide!" he shouted over his squad's barrage. "Radio the instant you locate cover. Jones, Robins, Donovan, drop back three meters and set up another skirmish line. We leapfrog after every ten shots. And DO NOT let them flank us."

The infected had been advancing on them since Finn's team responded to the radio chatter that the barrier surrounding the supercenter had failed. The instant the sun began its descent in the western sky, the monsters launched their offensive and quickly swarmed over soldiers and civilians alike, ripping them to pieces. Finn knew it was futile, but had radioed for reinforcements anyway. That was fifteen minutes ago. He understood help wasn't coming — they'd been abandoned — exactly as their new rules of engagement dictated.

"Sergeant, I'm down to one magazine," Jones yelled.

Finn's teeth gritted. He knew it would happen, but hadn't expected it this soon. "Switch to semi-auto. I've got two mags, plus one in the hole. Robins, Donovan, what's your ammo situation?"

Each soldier responded. Each had only one magazine. "Billings, SITREP! This is going sideways double-quick."

"Sergeant, I've got nothing but glass store fronts and locked cars with frightened civilians in them. I'm heading down Lakeview. Hold tight!"

Finn searched the area behind them and caught a flash of Billings disappearing down a side street. "We're bugging out. Head for Lakeview, and rally with Billings. Jones, you're on point. I've got our six. Move — now!"

With only Finn's gun holding the line, the infected pressed their attack and flowed unchallenged to his flanks. They would cut him off from his men if he didn't break engagement, and retreat.

Finn risked a glimpse at his team double-timing for Lakeview. They needed a few more minutes.

"You're not taking any more of my men!" he howled while clicking his M4's selector to three-round burst and digging his heels in. "Com'on ya freaks, come get me. Oh, you want some of this?" he shouted as a trio of infected broke from the pack and he destroyed their calves, crippling their advance. "Who's next?" he shouted, sweeping his fire side-to-side.

"Sergeant, what the hell are you doing?" Donovan barked into his headset.

"Find a hide," Finn shot back. "I'll break engagement when you've secured one."

Finn pulled his K-Bar free with his left hand and held his battle rifle in his right. This was his last stand, and he was taking as many of these bastards with him as possible.

He slashed and fired as the horde closed ranks. He was being swallowed in a sea of putrid humanity, but had to give his men a chance to escape. "That's the best you got? No wonder you're already dead. You're soft!" he screamed defiantly.

He flinched when a spray of cold blood coated his goggles off his right shoulder, soon followed by the thud of a headless infected crumbling at his feet. His team was trying to cover his retreat, but the dead were too close now. He'd never break free.

Finn's head arched back, his battle cry rising above the raspy longing of the infected, but then replaced by an engine's powerful roar. The sound so out of place it cut his cry short as it rapidly grew louder.

Finn's head swiveled, searching for the source. He found only twisted mouths yearning for his flesh. A stroke of his trigger sent two rounds screaming into the crowd and locked his rifle's bolt back. The end had arrived. His lips curled into a wicked grin. He'd always preferred hand-to-hand combat.

He charged the leading edge and halved the distance to his first target when the monster disappeared in a misty pink haze of severed limbs. Finn blinked away his confusion as gloved hands yanked him from his feet to the bed of a giant red pickup truck.

Bodies scrambled through his vision as he rolled atop dozens of crates packed tightly in the truck's bed, leaving his body even with the bed-walls.

"Hold on," a voice screamed an instant before the truck jerked backward. The smell of burnt rubber joined billowing blue smoke as the driver stood on the accelerator, wrenching the massive vehicle free of the horde.

Finn's body slid over the crates toward the cab, then tumbled uncontrollably for the tailgate when the driver slammed the truck into *Drive*, and showed the same enthusiasm for the accelerator and rocketed them over the sidewalk, heading for parts unknown.

Finn bolted upright as soon as the truck's retreat stabilized. Being pulled from the horde didn't guarantee good samaritans had saved him, it merely meant he escaped being eaten alive.

The tension released from his soul with a heavy sigh. He was surrounded by his team.

“It’s that group from the bridge and parking garage,” Jones said, answering Finn’s questioning stare. “And that woman you’re keen on is with them,” Jones added with a wry smile.

“Check yourself and one another for bites and scratches,” Finn said, ignoring Jones but cracking his own smile. “Do we know where we’re going?”

“Negative, Sarge. And I didn’t question them. Their little convoy showed up at the same time a bunch of infected rushed our position on Lakeview. I didn’t look the gift-horse in its mouth,” Billings answered as Jones checked him for bites.

“So, Sergeant *Helpful*, are you and your men clear?”

Finn craned his neck, finding Abe’s mug lodged in the sliding rear window. “We’re clear. Who do we thank for pulling our butts out of the fire?”

Abe winked. “We’re even. We can’t risk getting you back to wherever your base is. But you’re welcome to bunk in our community until you secure transport. Tell your POC...” Abe trailed off. Finn’s eyes had clouded over. “What?”

“I’ll explain when we’re behind the wire. But, hopefully, you have room for permanent guests.”

Chapter 36

Sergeant Blum set his radio down absently and drained the Highland Park Single Malt from its tumbler. The amber liquid was twenty years older than him, and cost more than he earned last year. "You chose the wrong profession," he mumbled, staring at the rainbow arcing off the fine cuts of lead crystal.

"Well?" Pamela demanded.

"Well — I'm going to have another drink, Pamela. And you're going to keep your mouth shut."

Pamela recoiled at being spoken to like a common street person. She found Blum's threatening-calm terrifying, so much so that she slithered into her penthouse, leaving the sergeant alone on the balcony.

Blum poured another double and sank into the patio chair's plush cushion. Seated behind the balcony's low wall, the apocalyptic scenes in Central Park were blocked from his sight. He marveled at the skyline, how normal the city appeared.

"Get used to this view. You'll be staring at it until you starve to death," he whispered, recounting the conversation he'd just had with CENTCOM. *Sorry, son,* General Malloy had said, *the Pentagon just issued new ROEs. Any persons, enlisted or otherwise, trapped, stranded, or left behind in a hot-zone are considered battlefield casualties. Understand, son, this is being done out of an abundance of caution.*

A scream, which waned in volume as it stretched on, broke his reverie, and drew his attention to the western skyline. The rising sun sparkled against a sleek black building, glinting off shattered glass racing toward the street below. Blum's head tilted, his brow in a tight knot, as the shapes leached from random, jagged plate glass, to flailing arms and legs. The form's gruesome demise obscured by the once bustling Plaza Hotel. He needn't have seen the end, a blaring car alarm painted that picture. "Death by deceleration trauma; a bullet to your forehead would have been quicker."

Blum gripped his binoculars and searched the ragged opening where the body had exited, and zoomed in as infected dropped from the shadowy cavity. "Chasing your food to the bitter end — I admire your dedication."

He swept his binocs across the horizon, interrupted by concrete and glass peaks and valleys. Blum leaned forward and rested his elbows on the low balcony wall. His view traveled northwest along West 59th, where office and apartment lights still burnt against the slowly rising sun.

After a quick scan down The Essex House's facade, Blum picked up West Drive and followed the migration of a pack of infected searching for shaded relief from the growing heat. The park grounds hadn't changed since he'd last viewed them two days earlier. Bloated, half-eaten bodies littered the macabre landscape while others pulled wrecked legs behind them, a snail-trail of bodily fluids marking their path.

“What the hell?” Blum murmured when a loop of infected filled his vision.

The mob formed a large ring around the edges of Sheep Meadow. The scene was reminiscent of a crowd watching a schoolyard fight with two forms in the center walking a slow menacing circle.

Blum zoomed in and his chest heaved, pulling in gulps of putrid air, as a tall, wiry man came into focus. His scraggly, graying hair faded into a lengthy, matted, crimson-stained beard. “You son of a bitch,” Blum growled. It was the man who’d slaughtered the young woman against the barrier, the one he’d nearly killed.

Blum snatched up his rifle and pulled it tight to his shoulder as he reacquired his target. His M4’s optics shimmied as he suppressed the urge to force the shot. He tilted his head back and swiped at the moisture beading on his brow. His target was over three hundred yards away. Although an excellent marksman, the chances he’d score a kill-shot at this distance were nil — a waste of his limited supply of ammunition. It would also act as a beacon to the infected still searching for flesh.

Several deep breaths later, Blum chose to observe the men, hoping to gain useful INTEL, and brought his binoculars back online. He zoomed in tight on the second infected. The man's stout, almond-hued features spoke of Southeast Asian descent. And his black eyes displayed the same unsettling intelligence as his counterpart. But he was distinctly different in two regards. His body showed none of the violence endured by the infected skirting the shadows — and he was smiling.

"What are you two doing?"

Blum rattled as the meaning hammered his mind. The delegates of the dead were communicating.

"Pamela, does this building have a basement?"

After a lengthy silence, Blum eyed the penthouse entrance with a mixture of suspicion and dread. The wildly annoying socialite never missed an opportunity to hear her own voice, unless she *couldn't* speak.

With a heel-toe approach, Blum brought his M4 to high ready, and entered the apartment with frosty determination. "Pamela?"

She didn't answer, but he was sure he'd heard paper rustling in the kitchen, just out of sight, and set course to end the threat. He smirked despite his circumstances. It wouldn't hurt his feelings to end the wretched woman.

His approach faltered when he again heard the rustling paper, then quickened before pulling short of the entrance. Blum tried to draw a mental picture of where in the kitchen the noise had originated.

His silent three count ended as he burst into the restaurant-grade space. “What the hell are you doing?”

Pamela’s hand, frozen at her mouth, pushed something into her maw as her shock faded. “None of your concern, Sergeant Blum,” her words barely audible through a mouth full of chocolate. “Go back to playing soldier boy. And figure out a way to secure my safe passage.”

“So, you have a food stash,” he said, glancing at the open cupboard above the six-burner stove.

Pamela reached up and slapped the cupboard door shut and moved to exit the kitchen. “The contents of my home are not for you to ponder or explore,” she hissed as she passed Blum on her way to the dining room. “Your only concern, *Sergeant*, should be my protection while you puzzle-out a way to deliver me to safety.”

“Does this building have a basement?” Blum growled.

“The domestic features of this building neither concern nor interest me and seem wholly unimportant to our survival.”

Blum stormed to his room and laid his gear across his perfectly made bed. Two full magazines for his battle rifle, one for his sidearm, joined his knife, gloves, NVGs, Camelbak, and a single MRE. It would have to do.

After topping off the Camelbak hydration bladder, he secured it to his back, then pulled his BDU blouse over it, chambered a round in his weapons, and bee-lined for the exit.

"Where are you traipsing off to, Sergeant? I believe continuing to shelter in place is the government's directive. So, unless you're planning to rendezvous with a rescue party, I suggest you remain indoors."

"I'm leaving, you're not. Enjoy your chocolate. I'll send you a check for the whiskey."

Chapter 37

Abe glared at Finn. The sergeant's words had twisted his gut. "What I'm hearing is we're dealing with two different strains of infection?"

Finn nodded. "Similar but different — yes. They can't prove it, but DARPA thinks both originated from some obscure lab in New York City. They followed the trail of bodies to that conclusion. But they've confirmed both were created by a combination of ant funguses."

"Ant fungus? Like zombie ant fungus?"

"Yeah, that's it. And they appear to have been administered differently, or so DARPA claims. How that was determined is above my pay grade. But somehow one strain got tainted — with opioids. The drug's interaction seems to create a more aggressive infection. They haven't IDed the original vector, or patient zero, but I'm sure CENTCOM is slapping together a suicide mission to find him or her."

"Seems counter-intuitive. How would opioids trigger a more aggressive physical response? Dumber, yes. More aggressive?"

"Abe, you're speculating on things I don't understand. Hell, I barely made it through the intelligence briefing. But the bottom line is what I told you. Some turned slower than others and escaped NYC. They have limited brain function. Enough to open doors, climb stairs, and rudimentary — wolf-pack-like hunting skills."

"See, that's the part... it's all wrong. They shouldn't be wolf-packing, opening doors, none of that stuff. Just easy to kill zombies, *that's* what I was prepared for!"

Finn's smile went crooked. "Well, I'm not a zombie aficionado, like yourself. But I've seen them do all that *stuff.* Some clumsier than others, depending on the fungus strain, but they worked around their limitations. Creepy shit, Abe."

"So, what's the plan? How do we beat them back?"

Finn rubbed his red-rimmed eyes and rolled his shoulders. "Can we finish talking tomorrow? My team's been running full-bore for a solid twenty-four. I need to catch a shower and some shuteye. Be here at sunup. And we'll cover everything I know."

"Sure, sure, no worries. But, one last question. How do we get you back to your unit?"

Finn's features darkened as his eyes locked on a distant memory. "We don't."

***

Abe parsed his thoughts as he walked from the quarantine house — his mind was on fire. *They weren't supposed to be smart or be able to move so damn fast.* "This is bullshit," he mumbled as he reached the sidewalk.

"Hey, we're moving as fast as we can, pal."

Abe pivoted to his right and found Ann's brother, Jimmy, glaring at him while his hand flexed around a length of steel pipe. "Relax, Jimmy. I wasn't talking about you. But that brings up a question. How much longer until you're finished?" Abe asked, gesturing at the partially completed fence surrounding quarantine unit three. "We need to make sure they're locked up tight."

"Tonight — we'll finish tonight. But I'm running out of supplies. So don't ask me to fence off any more properties. Clear?"

Abe nodded, but didn't speak. Three quarantine houses should be enough for now. And he really needed to get home. His legs went a little rubbery after his conversation with Finn. He needed to sit, mull over the information, and plan.

***

"Yep, they think it's actually two viruses or funguses. And I'll bet you a sawbuck we're dealing with two patient zeros."

Randy was quiet. Abe sensed his friend's tumblers falling into place. "Hey!" he finally exclaimed. "It's those guys we were watching on the videos, right? They're our patient zero thingies!"

"Bingo! And the government wants to capture them."

"How? Millions of infected are running around New York. And why, what good will it do?"

"Randy," Abe said flatly, "it's the government. Did you expect a common sense approach?"

"True. What else did Finn say?"

Abe took Randy through his and Finn's brief conversation, saving the bomb-drop for last. He feared it would spin Randy out of control, and it did.

"OPEN DOORS! Are you kidding me? You said they'd be stupid, Abe. Why aren't they stupid?"

"Hollywood said they'd be stupid, and you watched the same movies and read the same books as me. How's this my fault?"

"You insisted, that's *how*. I remember a conversation we had after watching *Fast Zombies with Guns*. I said it could happen. You said it was impossible because of the damage to their brains."

"Nooo, I said the stuff the guy put in the water would've damaged their brains and crippled them. And we both know firsthand they're fast, but not earth-shatteringly speedy."

"Jesus, Abe. What if they learn how to shoot? We're screwed!"

"Randy, you're spiraling. Take deep breaths, followed by rational thoughts."

"Abe, what are we going to do?"

"I'm glad you asked. Meet me at Stone's in ten. He's in quarantine unit one."

***

Randy laid his hand-drawn map of their neighborhood on the kitchen table. Its odd angles and poor scale had a vague resemblance to an angry kindergartner's doodle, but would suffice for the task at hand.

"Okay," Abe began, with unbridled enthusiasm, "Jimmy said he has limited supplies, so adding a second fence isn't an option. However, when we were driving to Stone's, I noticed, in certain areas, that someone had pushed anything blocking the street to the side. I don't know if it was intentional, but they created a metal barricade. Meaning, phase one of our plan is to secure as many abandoned cars as possible. Get them into place, drain their gas tanks, strip them of anything useful and weld their doors shut."

Abe glanced up, weighing Randy and Stone's level of engagement. Satisfied, he plunged headlong into the plan. "Phase two, eventually we're going to have to deal with human threats in addition to Zs. I'm thinking guard towers and obstacles between the cars and the fence. Like boulders, tripwires, and large caltrops. Then we fashion spikes out of tree branches, metal lawn tools, anything that has an edge, or can have an edge attached. Phase three..."

A knock on the door, followed by it creaking open, interrupted Abe and swung the trio's attention to the figure, backlit by the streetlights, standing at the threshold.

"Hello, Stone," Ann said dryly. "I hope you and your lovely wife are finding your accommodations — *comfortable*. I apologize for the condition of the house. I'm sure you understand.

We had to rush our cleanup and skipped the mints and fresh linens. But I guess it's better than living on the streets. We've already assigned you a new home for *after* you get out of quarantine."

Abe gulped a mouthful of air as Ann sauntered toward them. "Abe, Randy, do me a favor and tell me, what's the definition of quarantine?"

"Easy," Randy blurted, "the isolation of someone, or something, to prevent spreading a disease or infection. It can also..."

Randy trailed off. The sense of someone's glare on him cut his answer short, and he turned to face Abe. His friend's eyes were narrow and appeared to glow red. "What?" he asked defensively.

"It's a rhetorical question, Randy. We're not supposed to be here because Stone's quarantined for forty-eight hours. She's mad at us and now she's going to yell."

Ann smirked as she sat at the head of the table. "Oh, I'm not going to yell. I'm going to tell your wives. Let them deal with you mental midgets."

Ann held their gaze until she broke their will and forced them to look away. "Tell me, what exactly are you boys up to?" she asked, gesturing at the map. "Organizing an art festival? If so, the artist needs a bit more training."

"Hey," Randy mumbled like a hurt child.

"See, Ann, you're spitting nastiness again when you haven't the slightest idea what's happening. What if I told you we're working on our defenses? And we're doing it because our only concern is keeping all of you safe from the monsters roaming just outside our fence. We're unselfishly dedicated to preserving the lives of our friends and neighbors — because we care deeply for this community. Huh, what then, *Ann*?"

"*Unselfishly dedicated to preserving the lives of our friends and neighbors*? Lu wasn't kidding. You talk like a lawyer when you're bullshitting. Well, except for that last part."

Abe's jaw dropped open, but snapped shut when Ann raised her finger to silence him. He, again, marveled at the woman's commanding presence. The powers she wielded seemed equally mystical and unassailable, a powerful voodoo unique to her.

"I'm going to give you boys sixty seconds to say your goodbyes. After which, I want to meet with Randy and Abe *outside*. Good day, Stone. I hope this isn't an indication of how you'll conduct yourself while a member of our little *sanctuary*."

"No ma'am. Abe and Randy forced their way in and demanded I listen to their plans. I now see the error in letting them in. I'll exercise better judgment going forward."

Stone's gaze remained forward, avoiding eye contact, and in turn, Randy and Abe's betrayed expressions.

With an acknowledging nod, Ann sauntered from the house, her posture pin-straight and shoulders confidently squared.

“You suck!” Abe hissed as the door shut behind her.

“Look, when that woman crossed the threshold, the temperature dropped about fifteen degrees. I’m not tangling with that kind of mojo. I always thought you were exaggerating when you talked about her. You weren’t.”

“Abe, why does she want us alone? It has to be bad. It’s going to be *so* bad.”

“Randy, you whine like a schoolgirl — it’s annoying. We’ll just walk out there and take control. Seriously, we’ve been fighting zombies for days now. I think we can handle Ann.”

“No, you can’t.” Ann’s voice sounded like it rained on them from the sky.

“How’d she do that?” Randy whispered, his head swiveling, searching to see if she’d snuck back into the house.

“Let’s do this,” Abe said, marshalling his will with deep, calming breaths. “Meet at my house tomorrow morning, sunup. Finn’s going to tell me everything he knows; maybe it’ll help with our plans. But we’ll have to be stealth. Ann will kill us if we get caught again.”

“Your minute’s up. If you’re not out here in half a second, I’m locking you in!” Ann bellowed, scattering the men.

Chapter 38

Pamela smirked when she heard the echo of the emergency exit door slamming shut. He'd cover the distance to her private entrance hall in mere seconds. "Not even an hour and the *big brave soldier* comes crawling back to safety," she sneered under her breath.

A scuffle followed by a heavy thump startled her. Was he hurt, maybe bitten, and turning into one of those things? Pamela inched closer to the door, overcome with the desire to fill the shattered opening with anything she could grab. Her lips snarled, thinking about the damage caused by Soldier Boy when he'd forced his way into her home. The door he'd destroyed had been imported from Italy and designed specifically for her grand entrance. An exclusive creation of functional art, which Blum managed to reduce to splinters in a matter of seconds.

"You are no longer welcome in my home, *Sergeant Blum*! Leave this instant, and never return. I find you repugnant! Ah, ah, brutish slob with a tiny brain which I'm sure matches your manhood in both size and usefulness!"

An arid rasp, the volume of a whisper, trickled through the opening. Pamela shuddered. Something was wrong. Blum wasn't seeking to regain safety, but to take her life.

With frantic glances, she searched for a weapon and snatched a Versace candleholder from the half table next to the entrance and readied her slight frame to fight.

A muck-smeared boot slid over the threshold, eliciting her attack. The weighty candle holder arched above her head as she went to her toes to generate as much force as possible, the amount needed to force Blum to his knees, then beat him to death.

Her teeth gritted in anticipation of impact when her world suddenly became a flash of shapes and colors across her vision an instant before her head bounced off the marble floor.

Blinking away the red-tinted blur filling her sight, Pamela scrabbled for purchase, kicking at the hulking figure looming over her, desperate to escape her fate. A hand, slimy and cold, latched onto her ankle and yanked her back as if she were a sheet of paper.

“Please, don’t kill me, oh God, please stop this,” she begged as realization shattered her psyche. This wasn’t Sergeant Blum. This man, dressed in janitor’s garb, was here to eat her. He leaned down at an unnatural slant, exposing his nametag. Seth had claimed her for his own.

Chapter 39

Abe shoved Randy through the door then waited. If he dropped, Abe planned to lock himself in with Stone and Kat. His guilt was only a mild twinge; sure he loved Randy like a brother, but he loved breathing much, much more.

A peek over Randy's giant shoulders brought Ann into view, leaning against Randy's truck calmly awaiting their arrival. "Now I know how she knew we were here," Abe murmured as he joined Randy. "You couldn't have walked? You live two minutes away. I can see your house from h..."

"Abe, stop speaking and walk faster. You too, Randy. I don't have all night!"

Abe glanced over his shoulder, calculating how quickly he could dash back to the house when Stone pulled the blinds shut. "Coward," Abe growled.

"Abe!" Ann yelled, snapping her fingers. "Look at me, not your brother."

"What the hell, Ann? I'm here. What happened to nice Ann from the other day? I thought — our relationship was in a better place!"

"The other day, Lu told me what you guys did to save her and Nic. Today, I remembered who I'm dealing with. Plus, we need to talk — and it won't be an easy conversation."

Something was off. Abe detected a slight crack in Ann's voice.

"What's on your mind?" Randy asked gently, perceiving the same distressed tone.

"We've," she started then faltered before plunging forward. "People are running out of food and the pantry is already straining to keep them fed. Others need medication. Some want to go get what they need on their own. The news keeps talking about aid centers..."

"I'm going to stop you there," Abe interrupted. "We've seen what's going on at those aid centers. The soldiers in quarantine unit three are all that's left of the large force guarding the Rocky River aid center. None of our neighbors will make it. If they do, they'll bring the infection right through our gates. It'll be a shitstorm. Have you asked anyone if they have extra food or meds?"

"I did, with no luck. Everyone's holding onto what they have, and I can't blame them. We can't hold them prisoner. This isn't a gulag. But I'm at a loss."

Abe's brow arched. She wasn't asking for advice — she was manipulating them to risk their lives for the same people who wanted to string him up only days ago.

"When?"

"Tomorrow," Ann answered, a wry smile crinkling her leathery skin.

"How much longer will Finn and his team be quarantined?"

"Forty-eight hours, same as Stone and Kat. And no, you can't visit him tomorrow."

Abe's lips puckered as he chewed the inside of his cheek.

"What do you think?" he asked, casting a side eye at Randy. "We can ask Gage to join us. He's no slouch."

"We need more than three swinging..."

"Randy!" Ann shouted.

"Sorry, more than three sets of boots. I mean, we have to breach an entrance, clear the structure, locate and secure the supplies, and avoid getting eaten. That's definitely more than a three gun game."

"We'll do it after everyone's out of quarantine. But we need to talk about setting up a security force, a resupply force, even a strike force. If this is going to continue to happen, we need to train for it. And, the community needs to set up gardens. The people who didn't prepare need to start work on that A-SAP."

"What the hell are you doing?"

Abe flinched at Ann's boisterous question. "Damn, Ann. I'm standing right here and I..."

"Not you — him!" she yelled, pointing past the duo.

"The fence is making it difficult for rabbits and other small woodland creatures to egress to their natural habitat."

Abe spun toward the voice and drew a sharp breath. Stanley was kneeling next to the fence, pulling its bottom edge up and securing it with rope. The opening he'd created was half a foot high, and buckling the chain link above.

"Stop!" Ann screeched.

"We must connect with them. We must hold fast to our humanity," Stanley said, waving dismissively.

"Hey, if you keep doing that, my foot's going to connect with your ass."

"Tsk, tsk, such foul language from a lady," he answered snidely then returned to his toils.

"Abe, Randy, go put a foot in his ass!"

They were moving before she finished, and on him a flash later. With his back to their approach, Stanley was unaware of their presence until Abe seized him by the neck and yanked him away from the fence. His chokehold held fast to the man's double chin.

"Release me this instant," Stanley wheezed, his legs thrashing, trying to break free of Abe's unyielding grip.

"Sorry," Abe countered, "we Neanderthals don't listen so well. Randy, grab his legs."

Randy latched onto Stanley's cankles, pinning them to the hard pack.

"Ann, you have a captive audience."

Ann stalked toward the struggling man with a wintery glare. "Look, you pseudo intellectual bag of... if I catch you doing that again, I will tie you to a tree outside the fence and slather you in honey. If the infected don't get you, the ants, bees, and *small woodland animals* will. Have I been clear?"

Unable to speak, Stanley nodded and slapped at Abe's forearm. A silent beg to be released.

***

"That was some colorful language. I'm impressed."

"Abel, I didn't say the actual words." Ann grinned. "Tell me — what'll it take to pull together all those *forces* you and Randy were talking about?"

"People, Ann. A lot of hard-nosed individuals, willing to risk their safety. From what I witnessed at the neighborhood meeting, they're in short supply."

Abe watched clouds fill Ann's eyes as she parsed his meaning. "We're in trouble. That's what you're telling me, right? We're in deep trouble."

Abe's hand unconsciously stroked his holstered sidearm's grip, but he didn't speak as they walked back to Randy's truck. She wasn't wrong. The community would collapse if it failed to rally, to toss aside human nature for self-preservation, and accept that protecting the community was essential to satisfying that instinct.

"Put together a list of candidates. I'll take it from there," she mumbled, her eyes contemplating the neighborhood's way forward.

"I'll work with Randy. He knows more about our neighbors than I do."

"Of course he does," Ann smirked then peeled off, headed for home. "Maybe introduce yourself to your neighbors before I ask them to join one of your teams," she said over her shoulder, then stopped. "On second thought, don't. It's going to be hard enough to get them motivated. If they know you're involved, we're doomed."

Chapter 40

Sergeant Blum slid his night vision goggles into place and enjoyed full visibility in the dark, dank basement a moment later. Traversing the building's nearly one hundred-year-old mechanical room, he quickly realized that the building's owners had focused their updates on the luxurious living areas while patching together its vital systems. The boiler alone appeared to be original to the structure and barely functional.

When this thing melts, the results will be spectacular. His initial amusement with the idea of New York's ultra elite meeting a fiery death quickly dulled when he visualized the devastation awaiting the world as not only boilers, but nuclear power plants went full *China Syndrome.* "It may not be worth living though this," he whispered as he stepped heel-toe toward the freight elevator at the basement's far corner.

He estimated, based on the direction and distance he'd traveled, the elevator would dump him on 59th — inside the barrier. Unless something had changed in the days since the city had fallen, the narrow street would be stacked bumper to bumper with abandoned vehicles providing him ample cover from any nomadic infected not attending the convention of the dead in Central Park. From there, he planned to double-time to the GAP and secure one of a half dozen Humvees standing sentinel at the

GAP's useless security gate. He prayed the barrier's soft spot would fall under the weight of his Humvee.

His target came into view, its doors locked back, creating a shadowy opening waiting to swallow him whole.

Blum froze when his foot touched down inside the ancient elevator, rocking it on its pulley system. The softly audible clang of steel on brick resonated up the shaft like a muted dinner bell.

Every muscle in Blum's body threatened to cramp as he strained to hear if the infected had reacted to the sound. A swipe of his face against the coarse fabric of his BDU-covered shoulder cleared the tickling moisture, but did nothing to save his eyes from the sting leaching under his goggle's rubber eyepieces.

"Well, standing here with your thumb up your ass isn't a solid tactical decision," he said louder than intended. But the self-reprimand worked, unlocking his feet and driving him forward. He had no intention of dying in a basement. If today was his call to the pearly gates, he would arrive covered in his enemy's blood.

Blum removed and secured his NVGs, moved to the rear of the enormous car, then went to a knee. When the doors slid open, the daylight would temporarily blind him. If infected were awaiting his arrival, he'd cripple them with a full mag-dump, then exfil over their mangled bodies.

"You are a soldier, you fear no man," he whispered and grinned, his drill sergeant's words igniting the white-hot flame they always had.

Blum's hand flexed on his rifle's grip, his eyes narrowed, and his world slowed as he took his last peaceful breath before Hell found him. A rough bounce told him it was time to fight.

Sun burst into his eyes, pilfering his sight, but the enemy was waiting, their shadows brisk and focused. They surged forward as one grotesque organism, an impenetrable wall of flesh. Blum swept his M4 across the opening, folding the breaching enemy troops at their thighs. His boots were cresting the writhing mass the instant the last monster crumbled.

The morning air cooled his damp face, refreshing his soul and energizing his withdrawal. Thirty yards of bloody pavement separated Blum from his target, and its driver's side door was wide open. He couldn't have asked for more!

A chorus of barren rasps grew louder as he reached the building's corner, halting his progress. Pressed against limestone, Blum edged forward, and stole a glance around the building's edge. The scene roiled his innards. Hundreds of infected pressed forward, fighting their way into the building. He glanced skyward, visualizing the carnage taking place on the penthouse floor.

"Good luck, Pamela," he whispered, then pushed off the wall and bolted for the Humvee.

His eyes threatened to ignite from the chemical stench hanging thick in the air, but held their focus on the olive drab beast that would deliver him from this hellscape.

A flash of digital camo at the rear of the Humvee lit a flame in his gut. Had one of his soldiers survived the butchery? Again, the fabric slid from behind the vehicle then quickly retracted. Evasive tactics, that's what he was seeing. It was definitely one of his men.

Passing the vehicle's open door, he bounded toward the veiled soldier, and wondered for the first time why his warfighter hadn't tried to evac. Private Devon's ravaged visage answered his question. The Private's quickly blackening eyes locked onto Blum. At first, menacing, they softened as the youngster's forehead crinkled with sadness. He was sure Devon would have frowned had his lips not been recently torn from his face.

A stolen glance to the ground showed him the monster responsible for infecting Devon, a K-Bar buried hilt deep in its skull, and leaking the putrid fluff. This kill was fresh! He'd missed saving Devon by mere minutes.

Devon rasped, but didn't advance on Blum, instead he clutched at the mag-pouches attached to his tactical vest. Blum's stare widened. They were bristling with loaded magazines, and he needed them.

Blum's eyes misted, not from the noxious odor, but from Private Devon's hand raising to his helmetless head, where it stopped, then pressed hard against his sticky temple.

He nodded at the young soldier, snapped to attention, and saluted the hero, then sent a green-tipped round through his cranium.

His rifle's report drew the attention of the closest monsters, sending them on a stumbling charge for Blum's living-hide. With Devon's extra magazines in hand, Blum blasted the walking nightmares and darted through the open driver's door.

The Humvee's engine roared on his first try, and was racing for the barrier a tick later. He knew where to aim — he'd helped build it.

The eight feet of chain link between the barrier and the gate offered little resistance when confronted with nearly four tons of American steel moving at forty-five miles an hour.

Fishtailing onto Central Park South, Blum set a westerly course. He'd be slogging his way through the city for hours, of that he was certain. But estimated, God willing, he'd be home by the next sunrise.

Chapter 41

Su's skin rippled with tiny blisters which would soon blossom to festering pustules. It wasn't the cosmetic wounds which concerned him. It was what they represented — a warning to find shade before his body sizzled and shut down.

But he couldn't, not now. His soldiers were watching, waiting for one of them to fail. He had to show strength. Sampson appeared unscathed as they continued their faceoff. They'd been here for hours, circling one another, *discussing* an alliance. Su recognized his counterpart would gain the upper hand if he allowed their meeting to drag on. He now understood why Sampson's army held no reservations about hunting under the baking sun. They appeared only mildly distressed by its relentless heat.

Sampson's irrational demands and sputtering mind had hindered their progress. The fool actually believed his army deserved half of the city's hunting grounds. If not for Su, they would still be battling rats for the few meager crumbs discarded by the living while injecting poison into their veins — now they ruled the city, yet remained blind to the windfall a truce would yield.

Su's reasoning approach devolved to spiteful jabs over petty territorial disputes. He reminded Sampson his army had laid waste to the city, driving their quarry into hiding, then into the arms of the living fighters. Even now, the gluttonous rogues attacked the few remaining living hiding in luxury apartments, hell-bent on exhausting their stores with little concern for the months ahead.

***

Sampson broke a wicked grin, exposing flesh-packed teeth, when Su's arms began oozing bloody fluff. This man named Su was frail, unable to withstand the heat of day. Sampson and his army pushed past the sun's stinging rays, often overcoming their limitations by coating their flesh in their victim's blood.

Su spoke of compromise because he could not win, he spoke of hierarchy from a position of weakness, and spoke of the future because he could not exist in the present. He was leading his forces to the ruins where they'd be slaughtered while Sampson rebuilt his ranks. He would grow them to twice the size they were before the living fighters laid so many of his soldiers to waste.

Even now, his army feasted, while Su's sought cooling comfort, watching on in obedient subjugation while their hunger raged.

"*We will hunt where and when we please.*" Su's eyes narrowed when he received Sampson's words, then received Sampson's sputtering mind once more. The sound so similar to the clatter his newest recruits projected, he'd been momentarily confused of its origin.

Sampson seethed as his mind went black then filled with static like so many of his fresh soldiers' minds did. He needed to eat, to ward off the stammer overtaking the only thing tethering him to the power he held — his psyche.

Sampson's hands crooked to wicked claws as his mouth flared a depraved snarl. He would end Su, now.

Sampson's body coiled, abruptly ending their ridiculous hours' long dance. It was time to claim this city. He flinched, ready to unleash his attack, when an ear-piercing bang sounded in the distance, and the familiar pain of one of his soldiers being slaughtered pierced his skull.

Both men froze, then focused on the distant noise as their troops raced to punish the fighter who held the audacity to walk among them.

Sampson spun back to face Su, to carry out his assassination, but the ground where Su stood an instant before was empty. Su had escaped, leaving desolate earth in his wake.

***

"*Yes, it is secured,*" Seth projected in response to Su's question. "*We hold the high ground as you instructed.*"

"*And food? Do we have enough food*?"

"*We have... some food. The wild ones are trying to enter and may have found the other food. But we have some.*"

"Very good, Seth. You've done well; I am pleased. I will arrive at sundown. We will plan our conquering offensive then."

Chapter 42

“Don’t get so whacked outta shape, Abe. It was a good idea, just impractical,” Stone said, trying to calm his irrationally angry brother.

“It was, and is, a great idea,” Abe sputtered as he stomped through Stone’s newly assigned house. “As for *practical*, when did fighting zombies become a matter of practicality? I’ll tell you — never! It’s about survival! And survival requires bold thinking and creative solutions!”

Stone picked the neighborhood map off the floor, and smoothed its edges, thankful Abe hadn’t torn it to pieces when his meltdown started. “So, Randy, you say the locations of the wooded areas are accurate? And, before you answer, I have another question. Why didn’t you use a maps program to get a satellite image?”

“Yeah, Randy, why no satellite imagery? Mister Practical wants a clear representation of our homestead. He’s probably going to nitpick its symmetry and declare it impractical to defend!” Abe shouted from the living room then returned to sulking.

“Honestly, Stone, I never thought about it. According to the books and movies, we should have lost power, internet — tons of stuff by now, so I went with hand drawn. But, yes, the woods are pretty close to accurate."

Stone didn't respond, instead he focused on the map and pulled a mechanical pencil from his shirt pocket. After several painfully quiet minutes, he pushed the map across the table for Randy to review.

"This is what we should do."

Randy spun the map several times, reviewing the plan from several angles, then nodded.

"I bet it doesn't cover human attackers!" Abe grumbled.

"Yeah, it does," Randy countered. "It's a solid plan, Abe. Come check it out."

"Traitor."

"Stone," Randy began, ignoring Abe, "how do we get the supplies and machinery, or is where a better question?"

"Yeah, brainiac where *and* how?"

"When's Finn showing up? I'm thinking he'll be able to help us find most of what we need."

"Abe, you heard your brother. When's Finn getting here?"

Abe rumbled into the dining room with wall-shaking force, snatched the map from the table, then retreated to the living room. Randy glanced quizzically at Stone, who shrugged. His brother had been a hothead since they were kids, or *passionate* according to their mom. He expected nothing less. He knew Abe's tantrum would fizzle after he reviewed the plan. It was quicker and much easier to execute, and for all his shortfalls, Abe was smart. He'd recognize the truth. Plus, he made sure to incorporate some of Abe's design elements; his conciliatory addition would bring Abe to the table in roughly thirty seconds.

"Ah, I see you used some of my ideas. Smart move."

"Twenty-six seconds — new record," Stone mumbled.

"Finn should be here any minute," Abe said as he joined them at the table. "Your strategy isn't bad, Stone. But won't the dirt mounds offer human attackers cover?"

"That's where your tripwires and spikes idea comes into play. We'll place some on the enemy approach side of the mound. We bury spikes at random intervals, using sharpened tree branches, exposing about four or five inches of the spiked end. They'll blend with the dirt, meaning even if an attacker doesn't trip, a spike will find them if they use the mound for cover."

It was solid, Abe knew it, but he continued to probe for weak spots. His pride and neighborhood were on the line. He owed both a thorough examination, because he'd have to sell it to Ann, and be able to sleep at night knowing he helped mold their strategy.

"What's in the trench?"

"Caltrops, boulders, anything that'll slow an enemy advance by maiming or killing."

“Why so much space between the trench and our fence?” Randy asked, his eyes fixed on the map.

“That’s no-man's-land. Anything making it past the mound and trench will have to sprint across wide open, coverless, land — easy targets. Plus, we’ll string tripwires with spikes lined up for maximum damage. Same for the fifty yards they’ll cover from the main roads to the trench.” Stone’s delivery remained neutral. He knew showing enthusiasm for any individual part, or the plan as a whole, would send Abe on the offensive. They didn’t have time for that.

“And the wooded areas?” Abe challenged.

“That gets a little tricky. I’d like to see razor and barbed wire strung between trees and brush at head and ankle heights, keep our combatants off kilter. But the tree stands are key. We can use your hunting stands,” he said, dipping his head at Randy, “hidden by a butt-load of camo. Same for the towers inside the fence. It’ll be quicker and much easier to get them operational while we work on a permanent solution.”

“What about the gates?” Abe asked with growing intensity.

“Weak spots, for sure. But your idea of using cars or school buses, should help reinforce them. We’ll set up a double gate as well so we can facilitate entry without granting whomever we admit free rein to our community. The car or bus will be our first line of defense. It doesn’t move until we’ve determined the threat level of the person or persons requesting entry.”

Stone leaned back and braced for Abe's reaction, but a knock on the door broke the tension.

"That'll be Finn," Abe said as he pushed away from the table and scurried to the door. "Hello, Sergeant Helpful, nice of you to join us."

***

Finn wrapped up, and waited for questions, but only deathly pale faces greeted him. "I thought you'd have more questions."

"Um," Randy croaked, then cleared his throat, "white fluff bad, they're smart, east coast is lost, starting to show up in other states, and we may lose power and water. I think that's everything, but honestly, you could have stopped after the white fluff part."

"What's the west coast like? If this makes it into the homeless population... game over," Stone said.

"California's seen a few outbreaks, but has avoided the worst of it. They've halted commercial transportation coming from the east. They won't be able to insulate themselves forever. It's creeping across the country and people are fighting back, but the infected are relentless. Once they fixate, they attack until their numbers are depleted, or they likewise decimate the uninfected population. We've seen large pockets of uninfected here in Ohio. But the infected population is swelling."

"Are you still planning on staying with us?" Abe asked.

"Honestly, we don't have anywhere to go. Like I've said, if you'll have us, we'll stay. But we'll want our families with us."

Randy stared at Abe. He knew his friend better than almost anyone. He'd just asked a loaded question, and Randy waited for the angle to present itself.

"We've got room, you'll need to bunk up, but we'll make it work. However, we need your team's help with a few things."

Here it comes.

"First, we need supplies, a bunch of them. Adding you, your team, and families will strain what little resources we have. So we'll need to make a supply run. Second, I'm sure you noticed we're light on security inside the fence. We'll be recruiting bodies and they'll need to be trained. We're going to need some heavy equipment to build out our defenses. Finally, can you get us weapons? And I'm not talking about a few pistols. We need rifles, light machineguns, explosives, you know, *Army* supplies."

Finn tried to stifle his grin, but couldn't. "How'd I know you'd aim for the jugular on weapons?"

"Because you've known him for fifteen minutes. He's not hard to figure out," Randy said.

"I can help with most of that. You've got a deal."

Abe leaned forward and shook Finn's outstretched hand.

“One thing,” Finn added, holding Abe’s hand tight, “you mentioned something about a beer the first time we met. Can you help me out?”

“Sure,” Abe laughed, “it’s your funeral. But not until after our supply run. What’s your plan?”

Chapter 43

"Conductor for Three Southwest Chief. This is Terminal, Los Angeles Union Station. You are traveling in restricted space and your approach is over posted limits. Reduce speed and reverse course. You will not be permitted to disembark."

Peggy chewed her bottom lip, waiting for Charlie to respond. He'd been the Conductor on Southwest Chief for decades with a clean operational safety record. This wasn't like him.

"Three Southwest Chief, I say again, reduce your speed and cease your approach! You are not authorized to travel in California." Nothing, not even static — Charlie had seemingly vanished.

"Bill," she called to her Dispatch Control Manager, "Southwest Chief isn't responding, and he's coming in hot."

Bill flinched at Peggy's report. She was his best dispatcher, not prone to hysterical reactions. "How did he get past Topeka? How fast?" he asked while approaching her workstation.

"Topeka went down days ago. My guess — he didn't care, and tried to save the passengers trapped on his train. He's two times posted speed. He won't be able to stop."

"Send him to the runoff track."

"He's passed it," Peggy answered, her voice panicked. "We've got one option, but we need to act now!"

"Do it," Bill answered, knowing what she meant. "Derail them. It's a runaway. We can't let it reach the terminal. I'll call the National Guard. Stop that train!" He'd feared this would eventually happen. The terminals from Chicago to Flagstaff had been in disarray since the infection started marching west. Dozens of trains had sat idle on tracks for days on end, their cars brimming with passengers desperate to escape overrun cities.

Peggy slapped the derail switch and wept quietly. She'd just killed hundreds of people who simply wanted to find safety.

***

Charlie's masticated remains laid across the dead man's pedal, his girth just enough to fill the bell housing, and force the pedal to the mid-point. He'd been the last living human slaughtered by the infected; they were chewing through his neck before he even knew his train was in distress.

His final act, the one he accomplished with his dying breath, was to take his foot from the pedal and force his train to a stop. He couldn't have known the consequences his excessive weight would have.

The train's passenger cars hurtling toward Los Angeles had run dry of the living outside of Flagstaff. The once grand passenger cars now sloshed with gore... and the infected.

Three Southwest Chief, the largest locomotive in the fleet rattled parallel to Los Angeles' bustling streets. The unsuspecting souls going cautiously about their day, thankful the scourge decimating the eastern United States had, for the most part, spared them, hadn't noticed the train's excessive speed. Air conditioners on the unusually warm day masked the screech of metal on metal as the train's rail-wheels slammed into the derailer. But when the sturdy yellow device forced the locomotive's right side from the tracks, they became unwilling spectators to the carnage it created as the engine tilted on the track. Its wheels hovered mid-air, before the train's immense weight sent them racing back toward the tracks. The engine nearly righted itself an instant before the second car lurched and spun it from the rails.

Sliding through the debris-littered easement, it struck the closest tents and shanties with such force, they evaporated. Homeless in the distance, roused by the destruction, scrambled for their lives up the steep embankment separating the tracks from Alhambra Avenue.

Smoke, dust, and shrapnel exploded from the tracks, engulfing the Griffith Avenue overpass, sending cars and trucks into a panic for control while others plummeted to the train tracks below.

The chaos ended as abruptly as it had started. A gritty haze hung in the air before slowly settling to reveal a scene of apocalyptic destruction.

Zeke kicked at the tin sheet, which once served as his shanty's roof, until daylight filtered from its side, then tossed it away. Hinged at the waist, his legs splayed in front of him, he startled at the filthy soul staring at him, then realized with a chuckle, it was his reflection. His amusement quickly faded, replaced with confusion.

"What the hell?" he mumbled, watching his head tilt from side to side, trying to make sense of what he was seeing. A swipe across the image with his fingertips brought the sensation of sun-warmed steel. "I'll be damned, it's a train," his fog cleared as the pieces clicked together. A train had demolished his home, and those of his neighbors. "You lousy, no good, sons-a-bitches — you almost KILLED ME!"

Then a smile blossomed in time with the scheme budding in his mind, crinkling the grime on his drawn cheeks. *Amtrak is loaded. I'm talking deep, deep pockets.* "Show me the money," Zeke yelled, then slammed his face against the steel.

Blood splattered in every direction as his nose folded to the left and his head snapped back, dragging his upper body with it to the remnants of his shattered home.

The sun prickled his face, prodding beads of sweat to run into his eyes and forcing him into the fetal position where he noticed shapes moving inside red halos further down the wreckage. A drag of a tattered sleeve through his blood-caked eyelashes brought dozens more shadowy forms into focus. They appeared to be searching the countless broken bodies for survivors and moved with labored, stumbling steps as they navigated the rubble.

"Time to earn that Oscar. Hell, I'll buy the Oscars after my lawyers finish with your dumb asses. And all the women that come with it," he whispered, before unleashing a mournful groan.

Zeke marked their progress; they didn't investigate any single body for long, and closed on his position quickly.

"Help me. I'm hurt bad, real bad. Call an ambulance. I think I got internal bleeding!"

His plea reached the search party, scrabbling through the dusty haze, accelerating their pace. When he was sure they saw him, he closed his eyes tight, and waited to be saved... then the fun would begin.

Pebbles and rubbish pelted his face, kicked by his rescuers boots, but he didn't react, forcing himself to ignore their sting, and increase his sorrowful moans.

He nearly smiled when the sun vanished, blocked by his rescuers as they knelt next to him. Zeke opened his eyes and gazed dolefully at his saviors, and recoiled. "How the hell are you supposed to help me with black eye coverings? What, are you afraid to get a little dust in your peeps? Go get me some real help... sorry ass wimps!"

After his outburst, Zeke closed his eyes, reviving his starring role of *injured man on tracks,* and waited for actual paramedics to arrive. He stayed in character even as something grainy and cold tugged at his neck. Reasoning they were merely checking his vitals, he'd let them play doctor if it made them feel important. Besides, the shade they created was sparing him from the blazing sun. He'd let them play a little while longer. But his tolerance was wearing thin.

Zeke's scream never escaped his throat; it couldn't squeeze past the mouth clamped to his windpipe. He thrashed and twisted, trying to escape the searing pain, but more bodies fell on him, stifling his struggle. Some tugged his trench coat and shirts free of his body, while others plunged their hands into his pale, emaciated belly.

The stench of last night's liquor, mixed with bile, stung his nostrils as a single tear slipped from his eye. His life ended as he had lived, consumed by pain and violence.

Chapter 44

"Do you want to review my resupply plan or keep whining about what I said?" Finn snapped.

"Well, Sergeant Helpful, I just want to make sure you reviewed Randy's map thoroughly before you dismiss my strategy. That's all. So lower your hackles," Abe fired back.

He'd managed to interrupt their supply run planning session at least three times. Abe still, in his gut, believed Stone's plan was superior to his, but wanted to be absolutely positive the *professionals* agreed.

Maybe it was the way Finn dismantled his plan that stuck in his craw, or the laughs they enjoyed talking about the wall of cars providing cover for living and infected combatants alike. And he couldn't forget when Finn pointed out Abe's utter lack of forethought to storing the fuel drained from those vehicles. But he was actually leaning toward the fact, as Finn identified, that he hadn't counted on the large numbers of uninfected citizens, with guns of their own, who'd be rather displeased with a bunch of armed men and women trying to steal their vehicles. But he didn't fault himself for the oversight; he'd expected the planet to be dead already. The timeline just wasn't moving the way he'd expected, so some self-grace was in order.

Finn held Abe with a challenging stare, waiting for the man to continue. “Okay, everything out of your system?”

Abe nodded then waved at Finn’s map of the supercenter impatiently. “Stop stalling. Our neighbors need supplies.”

Stone glanced at Randy and they shared a knowing smirk. This was classic Abe, the master of deflection and projection. They’d watched him hone the skill since grade school, just over forty years ago.

Finn appeared confused, as if questioning who’d actually sidetracked their meeting, but quickly dismissed the thought and refocused on the map spread across the dining room table.

“This,” he said, pointing at a red outlined section of the map, “is where we enter. We’ll use the homes for cover, cut the fence, and then split into two teams. Team one secures the front lot and Humvees. Team two secures the structure.”

Finn glanced around the table. The mix of his team and Abe’s crew stared back at him. They were focused now that Abe had calmed down, but the entire situation chewed at him.

“After we complete our primary objectives, we’ll hit the medical tent, located here,” he said, circling the area with a blue pen. “It’ll be a mess. They weren’t treating infected persons. But it was packed with sick and wounded civilians. I’m pretty sure the attack started in there before the enemy launched their main offensive. We’re going to be dealing with some abandoned cars, mostly near the tent. Some may still be sitting in the queue we set up to bring supplies to their vehicles. We can use them as cover if needed. Questions so far?" he asked, then cringed — he'd given Abe an opening. But it was Stone who spoke.

"I've got supplies at my house, a lot of them. Do we want to bypass the supercenter and secure what I already have?"

Finn chewed on the information then landed on a decision. "We need medical supplies, a lot of them, as well as weapons and massive amounts of food. But, we'll definitely hit your house at a later date. Fair?"

Stone nodded. The sergeant was right. They needed enough supplies to sustain the community for months, not weeks.

"We'll collect weapons after we clear the tent and structure of supplies. If we have time and depending on our operational status, I'd like to search the roof. We had a team of snipers positioned as over watch. They may have lived, but roof access is located inside the structure. If we can't secure it, we load the Humvees and evac through the front gate."

Finn pulled a calming breath. The part he'd dreaded, the one he was sure would send the men into a tailspin, was his next topic. "Our team assignments are as follows."

The men bristled at his words. They hadn't expected this. They'd grown to trust the men they'd been fighting shoulder to shoulder with. Changing that dynamic wasn't sitting well.

"Stop and listen up. Team one will see Jones, Robins, and Billings," he glanced at Billings and nearly burst into laughter when he locked onto the man's pleading eyes, begging him not to assign Abe to his team, "paired with Gage and Randy."

"Oh, thank God," Billings mouthed as Finn continued.

"The rest of you are mine. We hit them at sunup," he glanced at each man before continuing. "We don't need a *Leroy Jenkins* situation. Remember, your individual actions impact every man standing in this room. Communicate, follow orders, and keep level heads and we all come home alive. Alright, get some sleep. I want fresh faces and clear eyes tomorrow. Abe, stay behind. The rest of you — dismissed."

Sergeant Finn gave a stiff nod when the group formed a huddle — that's what he'd hoped for. They were feeling one another out, getting to know the boots they'd be fighting alongside.

"You rang?" Abe said, breaking Finn's stare.

"I did. How much ammo do you have?"

"Enough," Abe answered suspiciously. "Why?"

"We — my team — have sixty rounds between us. I'm pretty sure that's not enough."

"Ah, got it. I'll have some for you in the morning. A thousand rounds enough?"

Finn's brow slanted. "Exactly how prepared for the apocalypse are you, Abe?"

Abe smiled. “I’ll have it for you in the morning. But I have a couple questions. Why not breach from behind the building and use it to mask our entry?”

“There’s a bluff behind the building, and they cut into it for the rear entrance and loading docks. With the privacy fence on top of the cut, we’re looking at a fifteen-foot drop. Nothing like a broken ankle to ruin a mission. The west side offers the best cover and clear sightlines. Next question.”

“When do we train our security forces?”

“*We* don’t. My team does, and starts after this run, and after we retrieve our families from Forward Operating Base, Ridgeville. Don’t worry, we’ll button up *our* neighborhood lickety-split.”

An awkward silence fell between the men and stretched until Abe broke it. “I know you’re worried about tomorrow, or more specifically, worried about *me* tomorrow. But don’t be. We enter as a team, we exit as a team. I’m not the idiot my friends make me out to be.”

Finn chuckled and grasped Abe’s shoulder. “We got this. I’ll see you at sunup.”

***

“Abe, go sleep in the guestroom,” Lu said groggily when Abe shifted roughly, yet again. “I’m working with Ann tomorrow. She’ll throttle me if I fall asleep during inventory.”

For the first time during their marriage, Abe offered no quip, snark, or off-color response. He simply pulled his overtired body from their bed and shuffled toward the guest room.

Midnight was fast approaching, and his mind was racing through images and scenarios of tomorrow's events — most of them bad, all of them painful. Sleep would be impossible if he couldn't burn off a couple of gallons of nervous energy, and decided he'd deliver the ammo to Finn's place. It'd give him some fresh air and a chance to clear his head.

"Solid plan," he whispered while buttoning his tactical pants and holstering his Springfield XDm. Staring at the pistol, he revisited every range day he'd spent with it, and ached for those days to return because, to date, the apocalypse wasn't living up to expectations, not one damn bit!

In the cool night air a flash later, he shifted the ammo can to his left hand as his right protested the weight it had been burdened with as he walked to Finn's home. He was taken aback by the number of lights still burning in the neighborhood at the late hour. He wasn't the only one suffering through stress-induced insomnia. "Hopefully, we find some Xanax tomorrow," he mumbled.

Abe pulled to a stop as he rounded the corner. Two forms stood just outside the cone of light cast by a streetlamp in front of Finn's home. The scene was out of place.

His right hand fell to his pistol's grip as he cautiously restarted his trek. The fence wasn't impenetrable, and he figured they would eventually experience a breach or two, but their movements spoke more to a casual conversation than bloodthirsty zombies.

After a few more strides, with his hand still on his sidearm, he breathed a sigh of relief when voices filtered through the sound of his heart thumping in his ears.

"Well, well, what do we have here?" he asked as Nic and Finn came into focus. "Two young lovers stealing away for a midnight rendezvous? How *sweet*."

Startled by the intrusion, Nic spun on Abe, raising her borrowed rifle to high ready. "Abel Andrew Willings, what the hell is wrong with you?" she shouted, letting the rifle fall to her waist. "I nearly shot you! I probably should — I'd be doing the neighborhood a favor!"

"Abel Andrew Willings? You're kidding, right?"

"Yes, Finn, it's my real name. And before you ask, I don't know why my parents did that to me."

"That's awful, really... terrible."

"Do you want ammo or not?" Abe asked loud enough to raise his voice above Nic's hysterical laughter.

"Yeah, I want it. But honestly, Abe, growing up, how many fights did your name get you into?"

“I can’t stand you, Nic,” Abe said flatly. “You’re like, like, a festering boil on life’s giant ass.”

Finn wiped at the tears flowing from his eyes as he and Nic’s laughter echoed through the empty streets. Without knowing why, Abe joined them. He didn’t find any of it humorous, but the sound of laughter, even at his expense, was like music. He realized he hadn’t heard a genuine belly laugh in at least a week. It was good.

Chapter 45

Abe vaulted from the truck bed the instant Randy slammed it into *Park*. The struggle against his urge to run between the homes and open fire on the infected rummaging through the parking lot nearly shook his six-foot frame apart.

"I've seen that look, Abe. Deep breaths help. Getting to the fight sooner doesn't end it sooner, it just makes it last longer," Finn said, gauging Abe's mental state.

He watched Abe suck in a deep breath, and was relieved to see the tension leave the man's shoulders. "Alright," he said with a wink, "let's get this party started."

Finn put his hand in the air and twirled it, bringing his team in tight. "I'm on point. Donovan, you're on my six with the bolt cutters. We do this exactly as we planned."

He glanced at his team, holding each in a momentary gaze. "Let's roll," he growled.

In column formation, at four-foot intervals, they reached the fence line in a matter of minutes. The homes surrounding them stood dark and lifeless against the rising sun. But Finn wasn't convinced they were as lifeless as they appeared. "Team one, eyes on the houses. Call contact if anything moves."

Finn heard team one shuffle as they set up a perimeter on their rear flank. He, not for the first time, worried about coms once they engaged the enemy. His team utilized helmet-mounted radios, which operated on a different frequency than Abe's crew's walkie-talkies. If they splintered on the battle-field, confusion would ensue and escalate quickly.

Abe, situated next to Stone, followed his brother's tense gaze to the parking lot's center point. A cluster of infected numbering in the dozens slithered and thrashed to reach the center of the scrum. "Something's got their attention, and I don't like the possibilities," Stone whispered. "Sergeant, glass the center of the horde, mid-point of the lot."

Stone glanced at Finn and found him already fixated on the threat. "What the..." Finn mumbled, prompting Stone to turn back to the scene.

"What's happening?" Abe asked, his voice hushed.

As one, the infected faced east as the sun crested the skyline, bathing the parking lot in its radiant heat. The outer edge scattered, moving shakily for the medical tent and store front as the trailing infected peeled off in onion-like layers until the source of their attention was exposed; an unidentifiable bloody pulp with jagged bones protruding through gore-soaked fabric.

"They must be starving," Donovan commented, adjusting his stance and gripping his M4 nervously. "I've never seen them eat anything to the bone."

"Agreed," Finn added. "They usually take a few bites then move to their next meal. But their retreat is what rolled my sack into my gut."

Finn glassed the area from edge to edge, adapting his plan. He'd expected resistance to be heavy in the parking lot as the infected probed the fence for weak spots to escape through, with only stragglers in the structures. To face their full numbers in close-quarters-combat was suicide. They would have to draw them out then hit them fast and hard.

Finn chewed on that strategy as he searched the lot for a force multiplier. With a team of nine, and the enemy split between opposing structures, they'd be overrun once the infected launched their dual-pronged assault.

He weighed scrapping the mission to regroup and focus on another target when his binoculars settled on a formation of three up-armored Humvees and a cargo truck abandoned near the main gate. And one Humvee, in particular, refocused his commitment to their mission.

"Change in plans. Team one, rally up," Finn said, then continued when team one rejoined them. "We need the Humvee with the Ma-Deuce in the fight. You're going to secure it and the other vehicles after we engage the enemy, and draw them to the eastern corner of the lot."

Randy leaned out of the huddle and locked eyes with Abe. "Engage," he mouthed while shaking his head.

"Randy, I'm talking," Finn said flatly before continuing. "You'll hold this position until they're moving on our location. Circle behind them using the tent as cover and double-time to the main gate, secure the vehicles, then snatch us up. Zip-tie the fence behind you. Team two, hold fire until we hit the corner of the building and get a bead on what's happening further east. If it's clear we shoot and scoot — leapfrogging across the lot. We've got a dozen vehicles to use as cover, but stay frosty. If the infected are using their undercarriages as cover, they'll be on you like stink on shit as soon as they see your boots."

"Sergeant, you've gotta see this," Donovan croaked.

Finn spun in the direction Donovan was staring. A single infected was bumping through the abandoned vehicles surrounding the medical tent, sniffing the air, and heading straight for their position.

"Shit... cut the fence, team two, showtime. Team one, stand ready." Finn's orders set off a flurry of activity. Men and their weapons moved into position; Donovan worked frantically to clip the chain link, and team two stacked up behind him.

"We've got this," Abe said to Stone from over his shoulder. "Stay close, brother."

Finn ordered them through the tight gap Donovan created. Once through, they moved in a 'V' formation toward the lone infected still sniffing the air, keeping the monster in their rifle sights.

Sergeant Finn signaled them to break right while he slid left as the zombie locked onto them and quickened its pace. The hoarse call to its food sent a bead of sweat down Abe's spine, but he never broke his focus on the fast approaching threat. It hesitated, shuffled left then right, trying to determine which bags of meat to pursue, then stumbled for the biggest prize — Abe and his teammates.

Through his rifle's optics, Abe had a magnified view of the sorry beast. Large wounds, oozing the grotesque white fluff, riddled its face and neck. That it was standing defied logic. When his red dot rested on its coal colored eyes, they seemed to glare at him as if his mere presence infuriated the monster.

The trio spread apart, creating six-foot gaps between them, and waited for Finn's orders. The zombie had moved close enough for Abe to recoil from the stench rolling off its body. His finger dropped inside his rifle's trigger guard. If it got any closer, he'd end the monster with a round to its forehead.

Abe's finger tensed on the trigger. He was seconds from taking the first shot of this battle. "Where's Finn? What are we doing?" he grumbled.

A flash of steel cut through the left side of Abe's optics, then disappeared into the monster's skull. Abe dropped his rifle to his chest as Finn yanked his K-Bar free, then pointed to the building's corner before spinning to lead them to their first waypoint.

"We've got movement," Donovan whispered harshly.

Finn threw his right fist in the air to signal a stop. "Location?"

"The cars. Inside the cars."

Chapter 46

Pinned to the ground, Blum shoved his gloved fist into the zombie's mouth. The monster gnawed furiously on the hard-knuckled combat glove, but the size of Blum's hand stymied its ability to puncture the thick fabric.

"God, you bastards stink," Blum yelled as the zombie's stench overtook the noxious aroma of petrol-stained concrete. Blinking away tears, he slipped his free hand under the monster's chin and forced its head back until the snap of its neck vibrated down his arm. Its body went limp, but its mouth was still deadly, and Blum kept his fist lodged in the beast's maw, using it to cantilever the infected to the side, and slip free of its girth.

From a battle crouch, Blum scanned his surroundings. The shabbily cared for grounds appeared quiet, but he'd thought the same immediately before the infected attacked him moments ago. The monster, sprawled at his side, rasped as its mouth chewed at the air. Blum pulled his blade and plunged it through the beast's eye.

"So much for being home in two days," he groused as he wiped his blade clean on the dead man's shirt.

He was three-days into his *two-day* journey and had only managed to reach Haven, Pennsylvania, leaving several hundred miles between him and his childhood home. He expected the hardest leg of his journey to be escaping New York City, then New Jersey. But, although difficult, it had been a virtual cake walk when contrasted with the rural cities he encountered along the turnpike. They were inhabited by people valiantly prepared to defend against the infection swarming their streets, and they'd made his life miserable.

In their efforts, they'd erected barricades which rendered entire sections of the turnpike impassible. The rare interaction with guards or militia were tense, and he'd found them inflexible when asking for fuel, a place to rest, or safe passage through their barricades. They simply ordered him to find an alternate route and emphasized their wishes to be left alone with large caliber rifles.

He gave up the direct path and picked his way through rural routes, stopping only to steal a few minutes of shuteye or scavenge diesel from an abandoned tractor-trailer or pickup truck. But this time, he'd thought he hit the jackpot, a vacant convenience store gas station combo on route 437.

Apparently, the residents of Haven hadn't acted as swiftly as other small communities, and paid dearly for their complacency. The streets were empty, save for the spattering of stalled cars with rotting corpses strewn around them. He assumed the carnage would only get worse the deeper into the city he traveled.

"Well, waiting for an attack isn't going to fill your tank," he said, moving to the pump and praying it wasn't dry, and still powered. His knees buckled slightly when the digital price glowed into view.

Power was one thing — gas flowing from the nozzle was another. The pump wouldn't unlock without payment, and his wallet was back at the camp he'd escaped, resting neatly in his rucksack with his cell phone, not helping anyone. "And dad said my job as a gas station attendant wouldn't pay off," he smirked as he approached the station's entrance.

Blum nearly jumped from his skin when the small bell above the door chimed his arrival, then recovered his composure and scanned the station's interior for threats. It was easy, the store had been stripped bare and its shelves toppled, leaving a clear view directly to the empty coolers along the convenience store's back wall. He'd hoped to find something to eat; he'd finished his only MRE the night before and needed some calories — soon.

"You better have diesel!" A sandpaper rasp seemed to mock his plea. "Where are you, ya skanky bastard?" he whispered, un-holstering his pistol and sweeping it left to right when a shattered cooler door burst open, spewing a grotesquely damaged man wearing a blue smock from its shadowy opening.

The infected surged toward Blum but tangled in the downed shelving two steps into its charge. Twisted metal latched onto his unsteady feet and slammed him to the floor. Sergeant Blum moved on instinct, closing on the monster in three leaping strides. Blue Smock struggled to right himself, and fought to all fours, presenting his greasy crown to Blum.

Seizing the opportunity to conserve ammo, Blum yanked his K-Bar from its sheath and, employing an underhand stroke, plunged the blade into Blue Smock's skull. The zombie slithered free of the blade and crashed to the rubbish-strewn floor, leaking the now ubiquitous white fluff from its ruined cranium.

Blum's head tilted, reading the monster's lanyard-mounted ID now poking from under its body. "Well, Ken. You've had a really shitty week. Glad I could end it for you."

Straightening to his full six feet, Blum gazed at his surroundings. The store's worn features spoke to heavy traffic. He'd of wagered a month's pay that, despite its proximity to route 437 and the turnpike, the locals were its primary customers. He'd grown to love towns like Haven. His Army tenure had seen him transferred to a dozen similar cities, maybe more. The people were always hardworking, no nonsense — heavy drinkers. *Kindred spirits*, he mused.

To his right was the open cooler door, to his left sat his target — the checkout counter where he'd find the pump override.

But the cooler door piqued his curiosity. He questioned how the clerk had fit himself into the cramped space, and approached it cautiously, squinting to see into its gloominess. "Well, I'll be!" he whispered when he realized a storeroom was located just beyond the darkened opening. "You must have sold a ton of beer to justify rear-loading coolers."

He glanced at Ken, taking note of the defensive wounds festering on the clerk's arms. "You died defending the beer, didn't you? Commendable, but stupid, ya dumb bastard."

Blum's stomach panged as visions of a backroom stocked with food danced through his mind's eye. It was worth the risk. Worst case, he'd find an empty room and then activate the pumps and search the town for supplies. "No harm, no foul."

K-Bar re-sheathed, Blum followed his Sig M17 through the shattered cooler door. Frigid air, pushed on his body by overhead fans, refreshed his stride and prickled his neck. His weapon-mounted light blazed through the storage room, countering the strobe effect created by the room's lone florescent light. "Like every horror movie I've ever watched," he smirked, glancing at the ceiling-mounted light fixture.

His boot seemed to glide on oil as it set down on polished concrete, but he held his balance, as he focused his weapon's light into the darkest corners of the room. "So, Ken, you died back here," he said, glancing to the floor to find his Danners planted in the middle of a thick puddle of viscous blood. "Oil would have been better!"

A long careful step freed him from Ken's bodily fluid and placed him near a four-wheeled dolly stacked waist-high with boxes. “Thank you,” he breathed, staring skyward when he found the boxes full of protein bars. “Beer drinkers — I love ya!” he said, glancing at two empty pallets littered with scraps of foil paper emblazoned with a dozen different beer logos.

Blum rolled the cart to the delivery entrance. His strategy was to fill his tank, drive to the rear of the building, and load the boxes into the Humvee. Pumping gas would be treacherous enough, no sense in drawing attention to himself loading up out front while completely exposed.

He opted to reenter the store through the backroom’s swinging door, and after a quick scan through its viewing window, pushed through. Blum cringed as glass crunched under his boots with every step; he was sure he’d never heard a louder noise and quickened his pace.

The ‘L’ shaped counter had taken a beating. From his vantage point, he could see the register drawer dangling open — the cigarette case had likewise been emptied. Gone were the snacks and trinkets present on every convenience store checkout counter nationwide. Replaced by torn boxes and discarded wrappers. “It must have been chaotic when they showed up,” he whispered, referring to both the infected and living.

The pump override was located exactly where he’d expected, next to the register and in front of the window. With a sidestep of a toppled wire rack, Blum slipped behind the counter and picked his way through ankle-deep trash. The override being his singular focus, he hadn't noticed his boot rustle through a scrap of blue fabric muddled within the heaps of brightly colored debris in his path.

Several key strokes on the pump override brought the beeping confirmation he'd prayed for. With one last glance around the store, he confirmed it held nothing of value, and aimed to leap over the counter and bolt to the pump. Shaving seconds mattered; he had a gas tank and two jerry cans to fill — in double-time.

His right hand planted on the countertop, he pivoted his hips, when his legs were abruptly yanked from under him. The sudden added weight, and violent shift, forced his plant-hand to shoot forward, sending the top of his body into a freefall which ended when his jaw slammed to the countertop, wrenching his head backward. As streaks of light shot across his vision, another vicious tug dragged him to the floor.

Blum blinked rapidly. The action didn't clear the fog from his brain. But the rasping call of the infected, latched to his legs, did. He whipped his legs around, trying to dislodge the monster crawling hand over hand toward his waist, its grip unyielding.

Blum sprang to a sitting position and pulled a sharp breath. The zombie now at his thighs had left a path of slimy fluids in its wake — its lower body had been torn free of its core. Distracted by the grotesque sight, he hadn't seen its open mouth plunging toward his upper thigh until it secured a mouth full of his BDUs, narrowly missing his flesh.

He pummeled the pathetic beast with his left hand while drawing his blade with his right then grasped a fist full of matted hair, jerked its head back, and shoved the razor-sharp steel through its nasal cavity, bursting its olfactory bulb, and scrambling its frontal lobe.

***

Blum hoisted the last jerry can onto the Humvee's rear cargo rack and nearly collapsed. His adrenalin had burnt off, and his body was quitting on him. He realized he'd be spending the night behind the station, tucked behind the steering wheel with a belly full of protein bars. It wasn't a room at the Ritz after a steak dinner, but it sounded just as good to his weary soul.

Tomorrow he'd search the town for water, and possibly a safe place to wash the death and violence of the last three days from his body and mind.

"I'm really starting to hate these bastards," he mumbled as his Humvee bounced over the body of the infected man he'd killed what seemed like a lifetime ago.

"You are a soldier. You fear no man!"

Chapter 47

"Lady, you're wasting time. If you want to live, get out of your car. We'll protect you. But if you're happy to die here, we're happy to oblige!" Finn whispered harshly. The woman continued to shake her head. She didn't speak, but the mascara streaking her face told Finn all he needed to know. She was paralyzed by fear. "Then drive through the gate!" She slapped at her fuel gage, a gesture the sergeant interpreted correctly — she was out of gas.

Finn peered over the car's roof, and watched Abe and Donovan deliver the refugees from the car they'd cleared to team one still waiting at the fence line, who ushered them from sight.

"Sergeant, we've got company approaching at one-o'clock," Stone said from his covering position.

Finn pivoted to one-o'clock. Three infected had braved the heat and left the medical tent. Their target was obvious.

His M4's stock made quick work of the car's window, spraying the flinching woman with safety glass. He unlocked and pulled the door open in a one fluid movement. Finn recoiled at the stench as the odor of accumulated human waste wafted from the car's interior. Controlling the woman by the scruff of her neck, he yanked her from the car and let her lean against him, her legs too weak to support her slight frame.

"Stone, cover us."

Stone moved to a blocking position, jamming the path the infected were traveling.

"Did my husband live?" she asked hoarsely, as her heels scraped across the blacktop. "He went to find water, but that was hours ago."

Finn bit down on the harsh response breaching his lips when he realized her husband was the human puddle in the middle of the parking lot. "I don't know, but we'll search for him," he lied.

Three shots signaled the plan had officially gone sideways, and he risked a glance over his shoulder in time to watch Stone adjust his sightline and send a fourth round into a growing number of infected shambling from the medical tent.

He jolted as Abe and Donovan raced past him on their way to reinforce Stone's position, their weapons coming online an instant later.

"Jones," he barked into his radio, "come get her and secure her with the others." He set the frail woman down gently, thirty feet from the fence. He didn't wait to see if Jones was in route, his team was in a fight, and he was hellbent on joining them.

"So, this is your brand of engaging? Not a fan, sergeant, not at all!" Abe yelled above the roaring gunfire.

"Meh, things went a little wonky, Abe. Don't make it worse by talking," Finn shot back.

“Left flank!” Stone yelled.

Finn hinged to his left and cut the threat down with a three-round-burst. “Move east, shoot and scoot style. Abe, you’re on point.”

Abe didn’t move, his eye glued to his rifle’s optics.

“Abel Andrew Willings, I said you’re on point. MOVE!”

Abe took three side steps, then faced east and moved like a man on fire. “I said shoot and scoot!” Finn called after him, bringing Abe to a sliding stop. His kneepad clicked as it struck pavement. From a kneeling position, he sent half a dozen rounds into infected legs, and was moving east the instant Donovan’s M4 went hot.

With a sideways gait, Abe tried to focus simultaneously on the medical tent and the store's entrance. At thirty yards, team two had reached equidistance to both, and stood dead center of the barren no-man's-land the opposing structures created — he realized he wasn’t Finn’s best choice for point man. He was supposed to clear a path and confront and overcome threats. But his forearms trembled, fighting the urge to empty his magazine into the horde. To make matters worse, his adrenalin had controlled his pace — he’d led them to the edge of their operational zone in a blur.

“Sergeant, I think I miscalculated. We’re going to run out of pavement any second,” Abe yelled.

Finn stole a look at Abe's position, then to team one moving with tempered fury toward the rear of the medical tent. They'd indeed arrived here faster than he'd wanted; he cursed himself for failing to rein in Abe's pace, but realized he'd been as equally amped as his point man. This tactical blunder rested on his shoulders.

"Abe, Donovan, cover the store front. Stone, you're with me covering the tent. Jones," he yelled into his boom mic, "roll ass to those vehicles. We've got a situation brewing."

"Roger," Jones replied, then hard-stepped into the space behind the tent. The structure's enclosed rear shielded them from the infected mere inches away.

The jolting appearance of a zombie, its face chewed ragged, stole Jones' breath. He couldn't fire, not with dozens of the abomination's brethren stalking on the other side of a canvas tent wall.

His fist went up, calling a stop as the infected rambled from the structure's opposite corner. It was closing fast, and he ordered his team to fan out, creating combat distance between them. The move slowed their enemy; it seemed confused by the sudden arrival of multiple targets. Jones watched its scanning eyes. It appeared to be trying to determine which of them presented the easiest meal.

Jones let his M4 hang from its single-point sling and eased his battle knife from its sheath. He sensed his team follow suit, but resisted a confirming glance. The infected was too close and wickedly dangerous.

The monster locked onto Jones. *Always go with your first choice*, he thought, adjusting the grip on his K-Bar. A parched rasp signaled its charge, its shuffling stride accelerated, then it plummeted from sight — an old-school, fixed blade, Buck Knife buried hilt-deep the cause of its demise.

"The ones in the tent are getting loud. I think they can smell us," Randy's whisper was barely audible as he slid his knife from his victim's skull. "We can't get caught jacking around with one while a couple hundred hunt us. Stick and move!"

Jones nodded as the rasping chorus surged from the tent. He signaled to move out when the tent wall flapped like a heavy wind had caught its edge, then ripped free of its grommets in zipper-like fashion. Its steel frame buckled soon after.

"Run!" Jones shouted, but his team had bolted the instant the tent began its implosion. The initial wave of infected tangled in shredded canvas and twisted steel then crashed to the ground, where the trailing monsters churned them to mash.

Team one rounded the tent's edge and blistered a path to their primary objectives, but the monster's reek stung Jones' nose. They were close, too close. The horde would overrun his team while they tried to enter the up-armored machines only feet away.

"Keep moving," he yelled, then slammed to a stop, spun to face the horde, and opened fire.

"SITREP," Finn hollered into his radio after hearing a distant M4 dumping its magazine. Then his gut clenched. He counted only four soldiers entering the Humvees.

"Sergeant, don't forget about my family." It was Jones, and his gun was rattling at full auto.

"Jones, come again," Finn responded. But his tightening chest understood.

Gage clamored into the turret and seized the Ma-Deuce. Her bolt was forward — she was ready to fire — he leveled at the mob swarming Jones, and slammed his thumbs onto the .50 caliber machinegun's butterfly trigger.

Arms and legs tumbled through the air as the gun's enormous rounds tore bodies apart. He needed to thin the horde enough to allow his team to exit their Humvees and enter the fray.

Billings punched the start button and pushed air through puffed cheeks. The 6.5 liter turbo diesel sparked to life on his first try. He was thrusting its brush guard through the horde's outer edges a flash later.

"Sergeant Finn. Jones was KIA. We're clearing these sons-a-bitches. We'll proceed to your position upon completion."

Finn's head sagged; Jones' first child had arrived last month. "Roger. And Billings — show them no quarter!" He knew the request was senseless. The infected were nothing more than eating machines responding to the misfiring synapses of their hijacked frontal lobes, but he viewed them as an enemy. Anything less would distract him or cause him to approach this war differently. Doing so would be a deadly mistake.

"Contact!" Donovan called flatly.

"What are they doing?" Abe asked as Finn and Stone repositioned to face the store front.

The infected had charged from the store, the action so swift and volatile, Abe questioned if the team could withstand the onslaught. But then they slowed to a stop before turning west to slink along the building's shaded facade, their black eyes glaring at the food just out of reach.

"Fire," Finn ordered, his tone perplexed. "Mind your ammo, target legs and hips. We'll mop up later."

"Sergeant, contact on your left flank," Billings' radioed warning startled Finn. He'd thought they had the horde pinned down.

"You crafty bastards," he mumbled, squinting against the low morning sun. The infected had caught them in an 'L' shaped ambush.

Chapter 48

Kat stared disbelievingly and chewed her bottom lip as Jimmy described the entrance to his company's grounds in excruciating detail. They were serious about the plan and possibly suffering from mental defects. Sure, Stone had taught her to shoot, and she was an excellent markswoman. But this... this *plan* was crazy. She cursed herself for sharing the map and notes with Lu. Leaving this type of thing for Stone and his insane brother to handle would have been the prudent choice. How, though, she ended up being a part of the scheme still escaped her. She'd merely mentioned the information, proud of her husband's efforts to keep them safe. At no point did she suggest or otherwise imply this group should go full-blown commando and secure the equipment.

"The backhoe is located here," Jimmy said, pointing to the north corner of the satellite image. "The dump truck, trailer, and tools are ten yards west."

"Any chance some of your crew took up residency on your property? Dead, or alive, either could be a problem," Nic asked.

Kat had once found Nic attractive, drop dead gorgeous, actually. But dressed in black tactical gear, she looked intimidating and hard. And Lu, her best friend and sister-in-law, Kat realized, was as equally unhinged as Abe. She'd been loading magazine after magazine while listening intently to Jimmy's plan like some kind of female Rambo.

"Kat," Ann began, nearly jolting her from her seat, "you've been awfully quiet. And ya look... well, a tad pale. What's on your mind?"

Kat twisted in her seat, trying to scratch an itch that wasn't there then glanced at each of them, locking them in a momentary, pleading gaze. "Well, I think you've lost your collective minds."

Ann raised a brow and waited for Kat to continue, but she didn't. The athletically built woman brushed a strand of flaxen hair from her cheek, cleared her throat, placed her hands in her lap, and stared flatly at the image hanging on the wall behind Jimmy.

"Whoa!" Nic bellowed. "That was a little harsh."

"Care to explain?" Ann asked, ignoring Nic's outburst.

"No, not particularly."

Kat fidgeted again; this time, however, a bead of sweat tracing her spine really was causing a tickling itch.

Ann nodded, but Kat knew it wasn't in agreement. Stone warned her about Ann, and Kat figured she was about to find out if the stories were true.

She believed the eyes were the soul's window. Ann's eyes showed a storm on the horizon, one she needed to outrun. "I just think we should wait until Stone and Finn's men get back. To be clear, I have no problem killing the infected. But there's only four of us, and we don't have the training Finn's team does. I've seen the infected in action. They swarmed over my neighbors in seconds, and multiplied just as fast..."

"Let me ask you a question," Ann interrupted, "when Finn's team gets back, how soon do you think they'll be ready to redeploy? What if they're injured? Or, God forbid..."

"Ann!" Lu shouted, flush with fear and realization.

"Days," Ann continued, skipping the rest of her statement. "You've watched the same government broadcasts I have. The infection is spreading — unchecked. How long until those monsters test our fence? How long until they breach it and start eating our neighbors? We don't have days!"

Kat fought the stress-twitch seizing her left eye and kept her expression neutral. "And if we're still alive, we can fight them."

Ann scoffed, and sprang from her chair, her finger pointed at Kat as she closed the gap between them. "I've had..."

A startling bang on the front door preceded Bina pushing through to join them with Lynn on her heels. The preteen searched the faces of her new community with downcast eyes. Her gaunt features and timid body language spoke to her fragile emotional state.

This entire group has gone mad, Kat mused, taking in Bina's tactical attire.

“I’m going to stay behind,” Bina said with a scarcely noticeable nod toward Lynn.

“Bina, we really need you,” Ann answered, glaring at Kat. “We’ve had a bit of a mutiny. Without you, we’ll never secure the backhoe or the other supplies at Jimmy’s place.”

Hold your ground, Kat urged Bina silently.

Bina’s brow furrowed as she glanced around. “Why? Who’s not going?”

“She’s talking about me, Bina,” Kat’s voice sprang from her throat louder than she’d intended. “I never said I wouldn’t go. I said none of us should go! We ought to wait until Finn’s team gets back. That’s what I SAID!”

An uncomfortable silence dominated Ann’s living room. The collective assumption was Ann would soon verbally assault Kat, but she, too, was mute.

“I may have a solution,” Bina finally offered, timidly. “Kat can stay behind with Lynn. I’ll take her place. But, weren’t more people supposed to join us. What happened?”

All eyes shifted to Ann. Bina was correct, the goal was to round up at least ten bodies for the mission. A point Lu and the others had been hesitant to address with the matriarch.

“Process of elimination,” Ann shot back, her defensive posture uncharacteristic. “We have to keep some semblance of a security force intact, which eliminated a large number of our able-bodied community. Others are working on projects to shore up our infrastructure. Some are too young or hindered physically. And here we are, this group," she said, waving her hand around, "it's up to us!"

***

Kat stared at the team as they exited the gate. She admired them and the grim determination each displayed as they drove past. But she feared she'd never see them again. It was a fool's errand pushed by impatience and fear.

"Well, Lynn. Let's go to my house, change into some work clothes, and then see who needs our help. Sound like a plan?"

Lynn nodded, a hesitant smile tugging her lips. "Sounds like a plan."

Chapter 49

The 'L' collapsed on them as if the infected heard Finn's words. Gunfire erupted from his side and his six, but wasn't enough... hell, they didn't have enough ammo, let alone time to repel the horde closing on them quicker than he'd ever seen these things move.

"Legs and hips," he yelled, but knew his team was already aiming for those very body parts. But they needed to know he was in this fight with them.

"Billings — sure could use a little support from Ma."

"En route, keep your heads low. We're coming in hot," Billings replied.

"Flanks, watch your flanks."

Finn dared a glance at Abe to see what had him in a tizzy. A group had detached from the primary force and was closing fast. "They're thinning our lines, box formation, behind me and Abe, NOW!"

Donovan and Stone repositioned while continuing to fire on the short side of the 'L'. Their new formation would concentrate the lion's share of their fire on the mass approaching from the building, while Donovan and Stone's guns strafed their flanks. Their formation was so tight, hot brass pinged off Finn's helmet and rained down his back.

“BILLINGS!” he shouted as the infected stench reached him.

“Down!” Billings replied.

Finn yanked Abe to the ground as Donovan did the same with Stone.

“Are you trying to get us killed?” Abe yelled as he struggled against Finn’s grasp. “Did you train with Bill Murray?”

“Army training, sir!” Finn yelled back an instant before the defining roar of full auto gunfire merged with the growl of diesel engines.

The sting of hot spent brass spitting from Ma-Deuce’s ejection port brought Abe’s arms to his head and forced him to watch the devastation from between his elbows. The first strikes shattered the infected ambush and threw hunks of their putrid carcasses skyward.

“Fall back,” Finn ordered as a haze of pinkish fluff drifted toward his men. “That means you too, Abe!”

“Damn, give a guy a second!” Abe shouted, fighting to a crouch while continuing to protect his head.

On Finn’s heels, the team scrambled to the opposite side of Billings’ Humvee and waited for his orders. Positioned broadside to the horde, Gage swept his fire back and forth, cutting down each wave the enemy mounted.

“One gun isn’t enough, is it?” Abe asked.

"You may be thickheaded, but you're certainly perceptive," Finn quipped. "Stone and Donovan cover our left flank. We'll take our right." Finn glanced to their six and found two Humvees idling mere yards away. His head cocked. It would work. It had to.

"Robins, Randy, reposition to Billings' rear bumper, then hold. On my mark, crisscross through the enemy formation. And try not to kill each other."

Finn waited as the war-machines rumbled into position. A thumb up from each driver set his plan in motion. "Gage, cease-fire. Team one — advance!"

Abe cringed as a cacophony of snapping bones and tearing flesh rose above the howl of straining diesels. Through his rifle's optics, he watched dozens of infected fall victim to the vehicles' massive brush guards as they churned through the gore with unrelenting savagery.

The apocalypse isn't going like I planned. Not one bit, he thought, swallowing against the sting of bile rising in his throat. A flash of movement at the building's corner refocused him. The infected were retreating.

"We've got squirters, east side of the building."

Finn adjusted his aim and caught a flicker of bright fabric an instant before a Humvee filled his vision. "Let's move!"

They cut a wide path around the butchery of the main battlefield, then set an intercept course for a small group of infected shambling for the fence. At fifty yards, Finn had reached the end of his last nerve. "Fire!"

His team did just that and leveled the monsters.

***

Abe's hands splashed to the gore-flooded pavement and stopped his rapidly descending face an inch above a glob of tattered flesh, but he couldn't stifle his gag. "It smells like they took a chemical bath and tossed poop and spoiled meat in for good measure," he croaked.

"It's definitely nasty," Stone agreed, wiping at the stream of tears rolling down his grimy cheeks. "You need to stop falling down. Get some new boots, for God's sake. And don't get that shit on your skin. Lu would never forgive me for putting you down."

"Put me down?" Abe questioned as he rose from the muck. "You'd kill me just for getting some of that crap on my skin? Even without a deep cut or bite?"

"Like a sick dog," Stone answered flatly.

"But you're my brother. Doesn't that mean anything to you?"

Stone's stare was as flat as his voice had been. "Randy, would you kill Abe if he got infected?"

"Without hesitation."

"Hey! You said you'd kill me if I even got some of that white crap on me. Not because I was infected."

“Tomato tomahto, either way, can’t let you drag this stuff home.”

“Live one,” Randy shouted before sending a 9mm round through its forehead.

“So, Randy, were you pretending that was me?”

“Abe, I’d kill you if you were infected. I don’t fantasize about it. But I’m pretty sure Nic does.”

“What about Nic?” Finn’s voice garnered a startled yelp from Randy.

“Jesus, Finn. Ya scared the shit outta me! You’re worse than my wife — sneaking up on me.”

“Relax, Randy. We cleared the store. Only found three more. You’re safe.”

“What about the roof?” Abe asked.

Finn shook his head grimly. “They went out on their own terms.”

The men were quiet for a moment, each visualizing that same scenario playing out millions of times across the country.

“Time to load up,” Finn said, breaking the tension, and cutting off his spiraling thoughts of Jones’ death. “We can’t take it all this trip, so the medication’s our top priority, then we’ll cram as much food in as possible. The ten-eighty-three should hold a month's worth, maybe more, of food, but we’ll definitely pay this hellhole another visit. Also, the civilians we rescued, they've gone AWOL. They're on their own — we're not searching for them."

Finn glanced at the trio. Dirt and grime covered each from boot to crown. They'd met the challenge head on. If not for them, he would have lost more than one warrior today; they'd of made any NCO proud. These men were exactly what he needed.

"You boys did good today," he said before turning to rejoin his men inside the store.

"Good? We did great! In fact, Sergeant Helpful, I believe we were the deciding factor in our victory."

"Abe, don't make me shoot you."

Chapter 50

Lynn watched her belly skin turn bright red, then pinch into the folds of the jeans Kat had dug out of a box of old clothes. "Not so good either?" Kat asked when Lynn's face crinkled and she flinched from the bite of rough fabric against her flesh.

"Maybe if I tuck in the shirt, it'll stop the jeans from squeezing my skin?"

"That might work. We also need to get some meat on those bones of yours." Kat scanned the youngster's slight frame. She'd clearly never been a heavy kid, but had obviously lost weight over the last week. "If it doesn't work, we'll just laze around the house flipping through magazines because I don't see any more clothes down here," she finished with a mischievous smile. Lynn was finally warming to her and breaking free of the emotional shell she'd built.

"Can't I just wear my regular clothes?" Lynn asked exasperatedly as she struggled to get her oversized shirt tucked in to cushion where the heavy denim was chaffing her.

"You know, I think it may be awhile before we're able to shop for new clothes. So let's try to keep the ones you have in good shape." Preoccupied with searching for another box of clothing stashed in the home's basement, Kat hadn't noticed Lynn's struggles.

"I look like a goof, but it works!"

Kat turned back to Lynn and went stiff.

"What?" Lynn asked, as she watched Kat's lip quiver before her own lips twisted.

"Um, well, you, um..." snorting laughter cut Kat's sputtering short.

She dabbed at her eyes, and tried to stifle her amusement, but then Lynn burst into hysterical laughter. The girl's two-sizes-too-big jeans were cuffed a solid three inches, highlighting her scrawny ankles. The faded denim then flared like clown pants before bunching tight at her waist, where the ensemble's thermal shirt ballooned. Its sleeves scrunched at her wrists resembled an elephant's knees.

"We've got to get a picture of this... you're a hot mess!" Kat howled, then grabbed Lynn and dragged her to the second-story bedroom.

"Go stand on the balcony," Kat said, rummaging through her things, searching for her cell phone. "The light's better."

The balcony was just large enough for Lynn to display her best fashion model prance, and overlooked the home's backyard, as well as that of their neighbor. As the pair vamped it up, Kat noticed her neighbor, an older gentleman, poking at the fence, but paid the coot little mind. They'd only been in their new house for a full day. But she'd noticed he was constantly tending to his flowerbeds or filling the dozens of bird feeders scattered about his yard. His presence outside was par for the course. She'd tried to introduce herself, but their brief encounter ended with him *harrumphing* his displeasure at her intrusion and slinking into his home.

A short while later, as the duo sat on the bed giggling over the pictures, Kat enlarged an off-center shot of Lynn's mug with her tongue hanging to the side and eyes crossed. She cursed herself for catching the crotchety old man in the frame, and began to edit him out, when something caught her eye.

"Lynn, honey. I'm going to check on something. You stay put."

"Where are you going?" Lynn asked, her voice rattled from Kat's sudden shift in tone.

"Hey now, don't worry. I'm only going to the balcony. I won't even be out of your sight. But, I need you to stay right here. Okay?"

To keep Lynn calm, Kat moved toward the glass-slider with restrained urgency. She had to confirm what she thought she saw in the grainy image. If she had, she knew what to do, and she'd do it without hesitation.

She reached the threshold, rested the palm of her right hand on her holstered Glock, and slid the door open. Her nose crinkled, the stench confirmed the worst-case scenario. Her neighbor had cut the fence. The picture showed a stray dog waiting outside the fence for him to finish, while eating something from the ground. But it was the lurking image of an infected, scarcely ten feet away, hidden in the brush, which forced sweat into her eyes. They never seemed to travel alone, and the crazy bastard had just opened the proverbial front door for them.

"Lynn, lock yourself in the bathroom!"

"Why, what's wrong?" Lynn nearly shrieked.

"Now, Lynn. Do it now. No matter what you hear, do *not* unlock the door until I'm back."

Lynn scrambled to the master bath, slammed the door, and curled into a ball with her back against the vanity.

Kat rushed from the bedroom and was bursting over the threshold in a flash — her Glock leading the way in a crushing two-hand grip.

"So much for Ann's security force," she mumbled while slowly approaching the corner of the house. The privacy fence between the homes should have kept the horde contained, but her neighbor had left the gate unlatched and waving in the gentle breeze. The same breeze carrying the overwhelming stench of certain death.

Kat flexed her hands to relieve the strain building in her forearms and slowed her pace. Her chest heaved as she rounded the corner. Her Glock's muzzle thumped against an infected nose before her second step.

Easy enough, she thought as she stroked the trigger and destroyed the bridge of the monster's nose. She dodged the pinkish spray with a hard step right. Her pistol screamed a second, then a third time, but only found one target. A calming breath settled her trembling hands, and the missed target quickly fell victim to her fourth round.

When the infected disappeared from sight, the breached fence came into view. Kat shuddered at the sight. More beasts pressed against the opening, fighting to squeeze their ruined bodies through the jagged gap. *Concentrate on their legs to slow their advance, just like Finn said.*

Her vision went dark at its edges, her focus solely on crushing their advance. The undulating mass, packed tightly together, forced Kat's sights to bounce in time with their rhythmic sway.

She released her breath slowly, then held her stance as still as her sparking nerves would allow. The trigger's pre-travel had just stopped when a pained battle cry startled her an instant before rough hands seized her arm and thrust it violently skyward, sending the round sizzling harmlessly through the brush.

The impact twisted her body and pivoted her feet, whirling her off balance. Her attacker, whose grip held fast as he tumbled to the hard pack, easily dragged her down with him.

Air whooshed from his lungs as Kat landed knees first atop his chest. Her free hand lashed out again and again until his grip relented and he covered his lacerated visage.

"We must connect with them," his muffled voice bellowed from behind his forearms' protective shield. "Enlighten them to their wrongs and labor to position them on an honorable path back from the abyss."

Kat scrambled to her feet and stomped the man's chest, silencing his psychotic babbling before wheeling to face the threat.

Three infected had pushed through. Tattered strips of flesh hung from their bodies, shredded by the jagged fencing. The horror of it worked Kat's trigger six times, four of her shots wasted — digging deep furrows in the dirt at the zombies' feet. "Stone would be so disappointed," she whispered as she blinked hard and refocused.

Her pistol's report echoed in the distance as she ended the triple threat, then shifted to an infected struggling to free itself from the breach where it had become impaled. The round pierced its skull, peeling its hairline back in a dusty haze.

Kat swapped magazines and released the slide lock, slamming the gun into battery. But her Glock's report still echoed in the distance... "Shit!"

She halted her charge after one long stride toward the gate when a wet thud from behind her vibrated through the stench-thickened air. Kat spun to face the lurking menace and jolted as the scene crystallized.

"I told you to lock yourself in the bathroom!"

Lynn white-knuckled a bloodied Warren-style garden hoe, and stared blankly at an unmoving infected sprawled on the muddy earth at her feet, the back of its head flapped open, its brain scrambled.

"He was going to kill you. I, I, didn't know what else to do," she said, her voice soft and fragile. "I wanted to help, but I got scared and hid in the bushes. Then I saw him sneaking up on you." Her eyes, when she pulled them up from the carcass, were doe-like and misty but hardened at the sound of gunfire from within the community's fence. "More got in, didn't they?"

"Get in the house. It's not safe out here," Kat yelled, as she inched for the gate.

"I'm going with you! I'm not locking myself up anymore." Lynn's forceful response surprised Kat, who was sure the girl's teeth would crack they were so tightly gritted.

Hectic gunfire ended the debate. "Stay behind me and do exactly as I say!"

Chapter 51

It's wrong, something's wrong, Abe sensed it. They were a block away from the community's gates, and he could scarcely see them. But it didn't matter. His roiling stomach and uncontrollable fidgeting told him all he needed to know. *Shit wasn't right*!

"What is it?" Stone asked. He'd seen this before, Abe was worried.

"Can't tell, but we need to roll ass."

"Last of your bacon go bad? Or did Nic eat it?"

"Why are you trying to make me mad, Randy?" Abe's frigid tone chilled the cab of Randy's truck.

"What's that sound?" Abe asked, leaning forward from the crew seats, straining to hear.

Stone tilted his head. "Randy, take your foot off the gas pedal," he asked, trying to lower the engine's rumble. "Shit... gun fire. Stand on it, Randy," he said, slapping the dash.

The F250 surged forward, separating from the mini caravan as the truck's massive engine roared in response to Randy's foot slamming onto the accelerator.

"Should we let Finn know what's happening?"

"We don't have a mil-spec radio, or time to stop to brief him. He's bright enough, he'll figure it out," Abe shouted as he checked his weapons. He'd burned through all but two mags for his AR and one for XDm, this fight would need to be efficient. "At the gate, I'll bail out, open it, and hang back to let Finn know what's happening. You... locate the shooters and radio me your location. Clear?"

"Clear," Randy answered, then skid them to a stop. "Go!"

Abe approached the gate with measured urgency swiveling his shouldered Ruger, searching for threats. His breaths came short and fast. The guards had abandoned their posts. He glanced at the latch. It was in place, and mercifully unlocked.

Dust pecked Abe's face and assaulted his eyes as Randy blasted past him the instant the entrance was clear. Finn and his men arrived seconds later.

"Shots fired, Randy and Stone are trying to locate the source. They'll let me know if they make contact. But we're not waiting around. Randy went north. We're going south. Make room!" Abe shouted as he clamored into the lead Humvee, squeezing next to Finn.

Billings wheeled the vehicle south while Finn radioed his team. "We've got shots fired. Gage, go north and use Ma to cover Stone and Randy. Donovan, secure the gate and shoot anything trying to get in or out. Robins, you're with me.

The supplies piled high in the Humvee's backseat shifted and tumbled as Billings turned a hard right and skidded to a stop when the bodies of dead infected came into view.

"We've been breached," Finn hollered, as much to the men next to him as the ones on the radio. "Gage, rendezvous with Stone and Randy, sweep the area then set up on the west end of the street. Shoot on sight. Robins, double back and join Gage. Set up on top of your vehicle and open fire the instant you find a target."

Finn shifted, trying to create space between him and Abe. It was no use. The oaf was too big and laser focused on the battle raging on the street.

"No, Abe. We're not running into the middle of that mess. I see *a lot* of people with guns. They'll shoot anything that moves."

Abe flinched as a hunk of olive drab paint splintered from the Humvee's hood. "That's what I'm talking about," Finn said, indicating the glancing impact of a stray bullet. "Billings, turn us broadside. We'll set up behind the Humvee, with Abe watching our six."

The men rattled and bounced as Billings mounted the curb, then backed into the street. The movement masked Abe's hard glare at Finn, but it didn't silence him. "This is my home. I'm in this fight, not on guard duty!"

***

Randy wheeled them onto the cross street leading to the scene of the battle. They'd swept the other area with military precision — it was clear. From there, they followed the sound of gunfire.

Randy regained control of his truck's supply-laden bed and redlined its engine, leaving Gage well behind and straining to match his pace.

“Hey, I know that butt,” Stone yelled when two women came into view. “That’s my wife!” He leaned over the center console and repeatedly slapped the horn.

“Your side of the cab, unless you’re trying to get us killed,” Randy snipped while pulling alongside the slowing duo.

“What the hell?” Stone gasped when his wife turned to face him. Kat’s wild eyes pierced her tangled mane; her clothing was smeared with grime and speckled with red dots, some larger than others, from her waist to her neck.

But the girl — her knuckles white against filthy hands, held a gore-smeared, pointed garden hoe at the ready. Her feral sneer and predatory stance spoke to a girl transformed into a warrior — a cold-blooded killer!

“What happened?” Stone asked as they clamored into the cab’s crew seats.

“That nasty old bastard cut the fence!”

“Which nasty old bastard would that be?”

“Our neighbor, Stone! How many nasty old bastards do we know here?”

"Yes, of course, dear. What was I thinking? How many got in?"

"Can't say. We killed five, maybe six. But I don't know how many slipped into the neighborhood."

"Looks like at least five," Randy interrupted as he fishtailed them to a stop, allowing Gage and Robins to flank them.

***

"I count five downed infected," Finn relayed to Abe. "But I can't ID who's shooting, or what's being shot."

"Yellow house, mid-point south side, second floor window," Billings said. "He's taking potshots then retreating. I've spotted at least three clusters of people behind cover and pinned down. What do you make of it, Sergeant?"

"Abe, get over here. Tell me who that idiot is."

"You're joking, right?"

"Do I sound like I'm joking? What's *his* NAME?"

"Couldn't tell ya," Abe answered, shrugging his shoulders. "Radio Randy or Gage, they might know."

Finn slid into the driver's seat and flipped on the vehicle's PA system. They didn't have time to piss around. "Man in the window. We've all been under a lot of stress. But this isn't the answer. We can work through whatever's bothering you. Toss your weapons out the window and meet me in your front yard so we can talk."

Abe spun at the sound of rustling bushes. His optics bounced in rhythm with a man carrying a hunting rifle and charging their position. “Not another step!”

“Relax, Abe. It’s me, Walter, and I’m not infected. But Steve’s wife is!”

Who the hell is Walter? Who’s Steve and how did his wife get infected?

“Just stop!”

Walter ran past Abe, ignoring his command, and his face crinkled with confusion as they made eye contact.

“The guy's name is Steve,” Walter shouted at Finn. “His wife was bitten and he doesn’t want us to... you know, do what we have to do.”

Finn’s hand tugged at his chin when it finished running down his face. They’d never get Steve out of his house alive. *Unless, of course, I lie!*

“What’s your name?”

“Walter, Walter Adler.”

“Does Steve trust you?”

Walter nodded. “Been my neighbor for ten years. He trusts me.”

“I want you to get on the PA and repeat exactly what I tell you. Can you do that?”

***

Robins inched forward under Gage's direction. The raw power of the Ma-Deuce would easily penetrate the home's siding. The challenge came in stopping the rounds from traveling through the house and killing innocents in adjacent residences. If Gage achieved the correct firing angle, he'd be able to send the round through the home's longest section and hopefully contain the rounds in the target dwelling.

"It's no good, Robins. I can't get a clear sightline, not for a fifty-cal, anyway."

"Gage, I've already got the window sighted in. I can take the shot," Randy yelled.

Gage ducked from the turret to ask Robins to radio Finn for permission to fire, when a shaky voice blared from the PA system in Finn's Humvee.

***

"Steve, it's me, Walt," the voice boomed nervously from the PA. "I talked to the military guys. They said they brought back a treatment — medications and other stuff. They can help Peg. It may take a while, but eventually, they'll cure her."

"You know that'll be a problem, don't you? Every person within earshot now thinks we have a cure," Abe said as Walter continued to talk Steve off the proverbial ledge.

"We'll deal with that later, after we get Steve out alive and take care of his wife." Finn held up a hand, cutting Abe's reply off as he listened to his helmet-mounted radio intently.

“Sergeant,” Robins began, “Randy has the window sighted. Requesting clearance to shoot if the target doesn’t respond?”

Finn pinched the bridge of his nose, hashing through the ramifications of killing a man for shielding his wife from an angry mob. As misguided as it was, he was protecting his family, as any man would. But Steve was a threat. “He’s cleared to shoot.”

The sergeant pivoted to face Walter. The man had gone silent, waiting for Steve to respond.

“Try again,” Finn whispered.

“Com’on, Steve, this is cra...”

The window, from which the ill-advised defense had been mounted, exploded as Steve launched from the jagged opening — his wife’s mouth latched onto his neck.

“Holy...” Walter yelped, his voice echoing down the street — pushed by the PA system he was too shocked to disengage.

Gunfire ripped through his resonance, sending Finn, Abe, and Billings scrambling for cover, as every person with a firearm unleashed on the couple while Steve thrashed and struggled to free himself from Peg’s jaws. Their carcasses bounced and joggled from the impact of hundreds of rounds striking from every direction along every inch of their bodies.

The carnage showed no signs of ending until Finn’s voice rumbled through the PA, ordering a ceasefire.

***

Randy poked his head from behind his truck bed and glanced at Gage. "That was a bunch of ammo wasted on two people!"

Gage, his eyes the only visible part of his body, shook his head. "We've got to work with them, get them some training. We can't have shit like this happening every time we have a crisis."

"I hope Bina wasn't a part of that mess." Randy swiveled his head, searching for Kat. He found her huddled over Lynn, a few feet away. "Kat, where's Bina?"

Chapter 52

"This is bullshit!" Lu yelled over the raspy growls of the infected. "Whose idea was this?"

"Don't start, Lu. We agreed, as a *team*, that we needed to get started."

"I don't know, Ann. I remember it a bit differently. If memory serves, you called me and *told* me we couldn't wait around for our *crazy husbands* to save us," Bina interjected.

Ann leveled a challenging glare at Jimmy, but he kept his eyes downcast. "Actually, Ann. I kinda remember it the same as Bina," he said, shuffling to the opposite side of the box truck's roof, as far away from Ann as possible.

"Well, *ladies,* you should have said something *before* we started our little adventure."

Lu tuned out the squabbling and glanced over the box truck's edge. They'd been trapped atop the truck's cargo area for roughly forty-five minutes — the temptation to jump into the horde and fight her way home... on foot, was becoming difficult to resist!

A stealthy tug on her AR's charging handle confirmed, for the umpteenth time, a round was chambered. Then, with a quick glance at the mud-pack below, she was reminded that the infected had trampled Bina's gun into the mire where she'd dropped it during their mad dash to safety. Of course, the dash would have been slower, possibly unnecessary, if Jimmy and Ann had remembered their weapons, which were now stowed safely in the backseat of Lu's SUV. She and Nic had barely fended off the horde and spent most of their ammo during the rolling battle. Nothing was going as planned.

We should have listened to Kat. She was the only one with the nuts to stand up to Ann. But if she were brutally honest with herself, Lu was just as geared up about completing this mission as Ann.

Ah yes, but your motivation was selfish. You did it for Abe. Your lunatic husband had been so far in front of this, and endured unrelenting abuse from me, our neighbors, Ann — and yet held fast against the slings and arrows. Oh my crazy Abel, even as we tore you down, you worked to keep us safe. You could have just fenced off our house, but you made sure everyone was safe. You just keep charging into the fray, and still they take their shots. Such a good man you are, bat-shit crazy, but a good man. I'm so sorry I didn't listen to you. But I need you Abel. I need you to save me one more time. God, let him hear me, please.

"They're pains in the asses, and certifiably insane, but good men." It was Bina, she'd joined Lu during her reverie.

"They really are," Lu said with a soft chuckle. "We'll never hear the end of this, but I don't care, as long as they come for us... they will come, won't they?"

"I'm sure they're *en route*, as they'd say. Geared up, I'm sorry, *in full battle rattle* and ready to fight. They'd never miss an opportunity for a solid *I told you so...*"

Bina suddenly lurched backwards, latched onto Lu, and dragged her to the truck's thin metal roof. Ann yelped and, with Nic's help, pulled Jimmy to join the fallen women where they lay.

The infected had begun to rock the box truck on its springs. They had grown weary of waiting for their food to deliver itself. They were hungry, and it was time to feed.

Chapter 53

"No, I said lay down, not climb down!" Abe yelled from his position in the Humvee's gun turret when Jimmy's leg slid over the side of the box truck. "And, if you think you're getting off that thing before your sister — and my wife — you're crazy! Be a man and sack up!"

Finn eyed the strategic position the infected held. The team's arrival should have pulled them away from the truck and opened up lines of fire. But the enemy simply spun to face them. They seemed to *understand* the situation; they knew Finn's men wouldn't open fire and risk hitting the food they'd trapped. The only good development was they'd stopped trying to shake their prey from atop the truck.

"This isn't good," Finn growled. "We've got to lure them into the open."

"They know what they're doing, don't they? They're thinking — strategizing. Son-of-a... this is bullshit! They weren't supposed to be smart!" Abe babbled, poking his head in from the turret.

"Sergeant Finn." Despite being positioned next to Finn's Humvee, Randy's voice sounded tinny and distant over the radio. "Who's going to *engage* the Zs?"

"I'll do it. I'm probably the fastest man here."

"Sure, Abe, you're like the wind, or a gazelle, maybe even ah, ah, cheetah," Stone said dryly. "*However*, I was thinking we just push them out of the way, like we did at the supercenter, load everyone through the turret, *then* we shoot them. No engaging or sending Abe the wing-footed-wonder to distract them. Just push them out of the way."

Finn cocked a brow while he stared at Stone when he finished.

"You're tired, Sergeant, that's all. We've been hard charging all day. Hell, we've been at this since before dawn and it'll be dark soon," Stone said, answering Finn's quizzical stare.

"Yeah, that's it — I'm just off my game a bit."

"Hey!" Abe yelled while snapping his fingers. "Whatever we're going to do, let's get on getting on. My wife's trapped and those things are hungry. Or are you waiting for me to take the lead cuz I'll do it? I'm not afraid!"

Finn craned his neck to face Abe. "How about you notch down your enthusiasm. We go blundering into this and..."

"Yo, Helpful, my wife's out there, so *you* turn it down a notch!"

"You boys have a plan? I'd like to, you know, *save my wife*." Randy's voice crackled over the radio, and he definitely sounded much closer this time. Finn leaned forward in his seat, and looked toward the Humvee manned by Randy and Robins, and shook his head.

"Oh, for the love... Okay, Donovan, pull up broadside to the truck and drive through the enemy. Slow and steady, and don't hit the truck. Randy, set up a meter off Donovan's passenger side rear-bumper and catch the castoff from his pass.

"Sergeant," Randy's voice sounded apprehensive, "how many feet is that?"

"Let's call it three feet," Finn answered, pinching the bridge of his nose. "A solid three feet."

***

Abe's knuckles threatened to rip through his skin as his grip tightened on the turret's metal lip. His urge to charge the .50cal and join the fun approached unbearable, leading him to cheer the attack from their position. "Carpe diem the day!" he hollered.

"Stone, are your brother and Randy disabled in a way I haven't noticed?"

"Sergeant, that's a hotly debated topic. Mom always called Abe *unique* and tended to talk to Randy slow and loud when they were kids. I think they're just excitable with minimal impulse control. But they'd crawl through broken glass to save their friends. I'd want them on my team regardless of their mental *deficiencies*."

The grisly sound of shattered bones forced through flesh as the Humvee duo made their second pass through the infected roiled Abe's gut. He hadn't planned on the apocalypse being this vivid. The sights and sounds would define his nightmares until his last breath.

Abe flinched instinctively when a piece of femur ricocheted off the turret's blast-guard, then he popped back to his full height, and glanced to the top of the truck. Lu, his beautiful Lu, her eyes dark with worry, tracked the war machines as they made their final pass. *I'll hold her tonight*!

Rapid slaps rattled the cab, signaling Finn that Abe was losing patience. "Listen up. We're going to pull next to the truck. Randy, Donovan, box us in. Once we've secured the objectives, we'll fall back. You clean up the stragglers. When the yard's secured, we'll load the equipment and exfil."

***

"Abel, get your hands off my ass!"

"Believe me, Ann. I'd rather kiss an infected, full tongue, than touch your ass. But unless you want to freefall to the muck, you'll have to deal with it!"

Ann glowered at Abe as they came face to face after he lowered her into the Humvee's back seats. "You're hot," he whispered, "but I'm married. If only we'd met sooner."

The power Ann generated in the tight space surprised him as her fist thumped his chest. "Don't be an ass! Go save your wife!"

Lu was the last to squeeze herself into the Humvee. She'd volunteered to help lower Jimmy from the truck. She let him go ahead under the guise of helping the aging man to safety, but Abe knew she was stalling.

"Well," Abe began, after breaking their long hug, "looks like you got yourself into a bit of a pickle. I probably should have warned you about these tricky, infected bastards. You know, after the first time I saved you. Oh wait — I *did*!"

Lu pulled Abe close and kissed him, then, with her lips close to his ear, whispered, "You're a good man, Abel Willings."

Chapter 54

Perched on the once luxurious apartment's balcony, Su grinned. The wild ones showed much fear for the thunder rumbling in the distance. They had devolved, becoming meek animals cowering from events they once paid little mind.

"*Bring me more,*" he projected.

Su glared at his soldier as he stirred lethargically. Seth's mind was dimming in time with Su's other early recruits. A development Su would soon be forced to rectify. But, for now, he needed to feed.

"*NOW*!"

Su's forceful prodding seemed harsh enough to push the witless fool to action and sent him stumbling toward the bedroom.

***

Pamela closed her eyes tight, the scrape of filthy work boots along her bedroom's hardwood floors told her the pain — the all-consuming pain — would soon return. It wouldn't kill her, only make her wish she were dead. She had abandoned her attempts to ride the pain to a place where she wasn't tied to her bed by the infected, being eaten alive one strip of flesh at a time. Her shrink was full of useless psychobabble. There was no *riding* or *escaping* pain through visualization. There was only white-hot, soul-crushing pain.

***

Su reveled in their hostess' screams; her fear would season his food to perfection. Eager to feed, Su rose from his perch. The change in perspective brought the entirety of Central Park into view. And there, alone in the expansive darkness of the park's ruined grounds, stood Sampson.

His confident posture unsettled Su as his nemesis' head tilted side to side, as if sizing Su up for a meal. Then Sampson simply broke his gaze and walked unbothered toward the subway entrance.

Su tracked Sampson, fearing the wild one would rush the building and threaten Su's feeding, when a subtle vibration raced through Su's feet and the distant rumble grew louder and more forceful. The air reached him in ever warmer pulses, and then the night sky screamed.

"Seth, secure my food, we must leave, NOW!"

***

A sound resembling a laugh rasped from Sampson's gore-encrusted gullet. Su would never escape the fighters. Their machines were too swift, their weapons too powerful, as they streaked across the sky. They would end Su where he stood. Then they would destroy everything in this city. The looming devastation had driven Sampson to plot their escape; the search for fresh hunting grounds had begun.

Sampson's pace quickened, the thought of finding unsullied flesh pushed him forward, when without warning, the night sky sparked with daylight. He flinched, his skin scalded by the flame from the fighters' weapons as stone shards speckled with green hued copper-works rained on his crouching back.

Now, to his right sat a smoldering heap that had been the city's crown jewel of hotels. The fighters and their machines had arrived sooner than he'd thought. His legs pumped furiously, speeding him to the subway's entrance where his soldiers awaited his arrival.

At the top of the stairs, he paused to glance at Su's fortress. *The man is doomed.* His thought punctuated by a reddish-orange flash as a single weapon ripped through the building's ground floor. The structure seemed to float from its foundation before it folded in on itself. Su's building was gone.

It's mine! All the food is mine!

Next From Bryan Dean

The Wild Ones: Abel's Apocalypse Book Two

Reviews are invaluable to independent writers. Please consider leaving yours where you purchased this book.

Feel free to like me on Facebook at Abel's Apocalypse. You'll be the first notified of specials and new releases.

ABOUT THE AUTHOR

I was born in Cleveland, Ohio and now live in NEO (North East Ohio) with my wonderful wife (she told me to say that). Cleveland is a great city, you should visit. But don't ask me to show you around, I'm busy and grumpy and will likely ruin your good time. It's how I roll.

In my early adult life, I spent time as a Repo-Man for a rent-to-own furniture company and bill collector. Then I decided that was a tough way to earn a living and spent twenty-seven years working my way through sales management in corporate America. I've always wanted to write books, and I realized that we, you and me, have about fifteen minutes on the face of this planet and I needed to do one of the things I had always wanted to do. And, well, this is it.